MAGNUS
THE RED
MASTER OF PROSPERO

THE HORUS HERESY®

The Primarchs

More Thousand Sons from Black Library

THE HORUS HERESY®
PRIMARCHS

GRAHAM McNEILL

MAGNUS
THE RED
MASTER OF PROSPERO

BLACK LIBRARY

To Ant Reynolds; for being this book's First Reader and convincing me to traverse the Atalantic Ridge to Merica.

A BLACK LIBRARY PUBLICATION

First published in 2016.
This edition published in Great Britain in 2017 by
Black Library,
Games Workshop Ltd.,
Willow Road,
Nottingham, NG7 2WS, UK.

10 9 8 7 6 5 4 3 2 1

Produced by Games Workshop in Nottingham.
Cover illustration by Mikhail Savier.

A CIP record for this book is available from the British Library.

ISBN 13: 978 1 78496 500 6

See Black Library on the internet at

blacklibrary.com

Find out more about Games Workshop
and the world of Warhammer 40,000 at

games-workshop.com

Printed and bound in China

THE HORUS HERESY®
It is a time of legend.

Mighty heroes battle for the right to rule the galaxy. The vast armies of the Emperor of Mankind conquer the stars in a Great Crusade – the myriad alien races are to be smashed by his elite warriors and wiped from the face of history.

The dawn of a new age of supremacy for humanity beckons. Gleaming citadels of marble and gold celebrate the many victories of the Emperor, as system after system is brought back under his control. Triumphs are raised on a million worlds to record the epic deeds of his most powerful champions.

First and foremost amongst these are the primarchs, superhuman beings who have led the Space Marine Legions in campaign after campaign. They are unstoppable and magnificent, the pinnacle of the Emperor's genetic experimentation, while the Space Marines themselves are the mightiest human warriors the galaxy has ever known, each capable of besting a hundred normal men or more in combat.

Many are the tales told of these legendary beings. From the halls of the Imperial Palace on Terra to the outermost reaches of Ultima Segmentum, their deeds are known to be shaping the very future of the galaxy. But can such souls remain free of doubt and corruption forever? Or will the temptation of greater power prove too much for even the most loyal sons of the Emperor?

The seeds of heresy have already been sown, and the start of the greatest war in the history of mankind is but a few years away...

'Wisdom comes from remembering the past and taking responsibility for the future.'

– Preface to the *Book of Magnus*

'Give me a lever long enough, and a fulcrum upon which to place it, and I shall move the world.'

– from *The Apologues of Olympia,*
by the primarch Perturabo

The Planet of the Sorcerers
Time unknown

Magnus did not know this place.

Not as it was now.

He remembered the Pyramid of Photep as a place of light, of polished glass and dazzling reflections. A place where star-beams and sunlight made sport on the earth below.

Beautiful people had once gathered within its golden-vaulted atria, holding impassioned debates on ethics, morality and virtue. They once delighted in the knowledge that their world was founded on principles of reason, wisdom and the pursuit of higher truths.

Now its interior was cold and lifeless, home only to mutter-ing shadows and broken glass reflections he dared not heed. Its fellow pyramids of the Fellowships were sagging ruins of charred-black adamantium, hollowed out skeletons adrift in a dust-choked wasteland.

Lightning danced on the horizon beyond the pyramids, their broken framework throwing stark shadows around him. Mag-nus took a moment to orient himself. Once he would have known exactly where to go, but times had changed.

The frames of the pyramids had buckled in the heat of their

burning, but it had been the translation from Prospero to this protean world that rendered every one of them into something hideously deformed. Their angles, once so true, were twisted unnaturally, as if to mock their perfect forms.

He looked up into the echoing void, picturing his final battle with the Wolf King. Sadness welled within him at the memory. Two brothers, opposites in many ways, yet so alike at their fundamental levels. How different it might have been.

The dust swirled above Magnus, forming a hazy image of that moment, and he averted his gaze, unwilling to relive his deepest shame once more.

That his world had been razed was a cut to the heart that would never heal, but the Pyramid of Photep's loss was the deepest wound of all.

One of the wonders of the galaxy, it had been his sanctum sanctorum, the representation of all that was great and noble on Prospero. It had contained his greatest treasures: texts dating back to mankind's first impressions on clay; its blind, stumbling strides into science and philosophy; its great dramatic literature, and irreplaceable works of art.

All gone, burned in a single night of unimaginable violence.

The night his father unleashed the wolves of Fenris.

They had howled and raged at the moon.

They had feasted well.

But they had failed.

Magnus and his Thousand Sons had escaped, borne through the howling chaos of the Great Ocean to this world of madness. He had never seen this planet before, never known or suspected its existence, but he knew its name as well as his own.

The Planet of the Sorcerers.

An apposite name, for power coursed through every one of his sons that remained.

Power that might soon destroy them all.

Magnus picked a path through the wreckage, a numinous angel amid the ashes of his guilt. His corporeal body had been sundered across the knee of the Wolf King, but this new flesh – fashioned of warp matter – was as solid as it had been in life. But what had that transition done to his soul? What had he become?

He did not yet know.

A ghost? A memory given form?

Or the purest expression of his true nature?

Debris choked the interior of the pyramid, and he stepped over towering bookcases toppled like the mightiest trees of the forest and data-crystals crushed beneath Fenrisian boots. Fluttering pages of ashen grimoires drifted on the mournful wind, and Magnus plucked one from the air.

He recognised it. Of course he did – there wasn't a tome on Prospero he couldn't recall.

Indeed, it is a strange disposed time:
But men may construe things after their fashion,
Clean from the purpose of the things themselves.

One of the plays penned by the famed dramaturge of Albia. Even among all the great works of architecture, mathematics and science that lay in ashes around him, this loss struck Magnus deeply. Great works of technology could always be rediscovered, but works of art were unique and would never come again.

Magnus went down on one knee and splayed his fingers in the dust, letting the power of the Great Ocean flow through him. He drew the memory of the ancient wordsmith's art from within the halls of his memory. Glittering motes of golden light rose like fireflies from the ash. They drifted around him, spiralling in a double helix pattern and flowing into the scrap of paper.

Like a conflagration in reverse, the page reformed. Magnus smiled with pleasure as the motes of light conjoined around the remaining page, forming others in a rush of newly wrought parchment. He closed his eye and let out a breath that was not truly breath, feeling the same joy as the play's mysterious creator must have felt as he first scratched the words into existence.

Magnus felt weight settle in his palm and opened his eye. The manuscript was complete, the words glistening on the page as though fresh-inked.

'Do you plan to restore everything you lost like that?'

'If I have to,' said Magnus.

'It won't work.'

'And you know this how?'

'Because I know what you know,' said the unseen speaker, 'and *you* know it won't work. But you'll try anyway.'

Magnus rose to his full height and turned, letting memory clothe him in the war-plate he had worn on Prospero's last day: burnished gold with curling horns, pteruges of boiled leather and a wild mane of crimson hair bound with a bronze circlet.

Before him stood a black-robed figure with the unmistakable bulk of a legionary. His hands were laced before him at his waist, and a golden Crusader ring glittered on the middle finger of his right hand. His features were handsomely clean-cut, and his long black hair, severely swept back over a tapered skull, gave him a hawkish aspect.

'I have not thought of that face in an age,' said Magnus, resting a hand on the red leather cover of his eponymous book.

'Lie to me and you only deceive yourself,' said the legionary. 'Remember, I know what you know.'

'Very well,' said the primarch. 'Then let us say that I *try* not to think of him.'

The figure circled Magnus, studying him as though they were

newly reunited acquaintances. The notion was not completely absurd.

'He remembers the first time he saw you like that,' said the legionary. 'He was almost dead and thought you a vision come to usher him into the beyond.'

'I remember it well,' said Magnus. 'I am surprised *he* does.'

The legionary opened his hands and grinned. 'Maybe I remember *you* remembering it, or maybe I read it in the pages of your grand grimoire. Either way, he was not himself back then. Few of you were. But you fixed them, didn't you? Just like you fixed us.'

'I tried,' said Magnus, walking deeper into the ruins of the pyramid. 'I tried so hard to save all my sons.'

The legionary followed him. 'I know you did,' he said, 'but your cure was worse than the disease.'

'You think I do not know that?' snapped Magnus, following a spiralling path towards a wide shell crater filled with razored shards of glass. 'What choice did I have?'

'You could have let them die.'

'Never. They were my sons!'

'But what are they now?' asked the figure, descending into the crater. 'And what will they become? Look into the Great Ocean, Magnus. Read the tides of the future and tell me if you still feel pride at their deeds in all the centuries to come.'

'No!' cried Magnus, stumbling down into the crater, all thoughts of regret and shame pushed aside by anger. Glass cracked underfoot, ten thousand reflections staring back at him in silent accusation.

No two were alike, each facet an aspect of his soul he dared not confront.

'The future is not set,' said Magnus. 'Horus fell into the trap of believing that on Davin. I will not make the same mistake.'

'No, you will make new ones,' said the figure, tapping a finger against his forehead. Magnus felt his gaze drawn to the legionary's golden ring. The motif worked into the metal was unclear, but he did not need to see it to know what it was or understand the guilt of what it represented.

'You will make worse mistakes because you still believe you can fix everything,' continued the legionary. 'The all-powerful Magnus – *he* can save everyone, because he is cleverer than anyone else. He knows things no one else knows.'

'That face you wear? He cannot be here,' said Magnus. 'My brother killed him on Terra.'

'So?' asked the legionary. 'You know better than anyone that the death of the matter binding our souls to this existence means nothing. *Less* than nothing on a world like this.'

'I felt him let go of his silver cord.'

'But you were the one who cut it,' the legionary reminded him, holding up his ring so Magnus could see the eagle and crossed lightning bolts worked upon its surface. 'You were the one who sent him back to Terra as a symbol, too broken to serve at the forefront of the Great Crusade.'

'Russ smote me far worse than I suspected,' said Magnus. 'My mind is unravelling.'

'There's truth in that, too, but you know I am not a figment of your disintegrating mind. I come bearing a warning.'

'A warning?' said Magnus, taking a step towards the legionary and drawing the destructive power of the Great Ocean into his fists. 'What warning do you bear?'

'Only what you already know – that the powers you bartered with have not finished with you and your sons. There is a price yet to pay for past misdeeds.'

Magnus laughed, a bitter bark freighted with boundless regret and unending sorrow.

'What more can the Primordial Annihilator take from me?' said Magnus, sinking to his knees and lifting handfuls of broken glass and dust. 'The Wolves razed my world and burned our knowledge to ash! My sons are dying and I am helpless to save them!'

'Magnus the Red, the Crimson King, *helpless?* No, you don't really believe that or you wouldn't be here.'

Magnus let the glass and dust spill from his hands as he saw the gleam of partially exposed metal beneath him.

'There is still a way to cheat your fate,' said the dead legionary.

'How?'

'You remember Morningstar?'

'Yes, Atharva,' said Magnus. 'I remember Morningstar.'

MORNINGSTAR, 853.M30

THE FIFTY-FIFTH YEAR OF THE GREAT CRUSADE

Category 8: DISASTER
[Large scale and duration – localised populated area]

Ω

ONE

ZHARRUKIN • MASTER OF THE SONS • LORD OF IRON

The dust swirled like a miniature vortex in Atharva's palm, its composite elements spun by the whims of the planet's increasingly chaotic magnetic fields. It was reckless to remain in Zharrukin's ruins in the face of the oncoming magna-storm, but the Thousand Sons did not lightly abandon knowledge won by lost generations.

An ashen wind howled through the broken structures and collapsed ruins, as if in lament for the city's lost glories. It must once have been magnificent, the scale and plan of the remaining stumps of pitted marble suggestive of enormous constructions of polished stone and shimmering glass.

Zharrukin spread from the rugged haunches of the mountains, following the unnaturally straight groove of a wide river valley. A thousand years or more had passed since the city had been inhabited, and nature had reclaimed many of its ancient plascrete canyons and shattered thoroughfares.

The architecture was pre-Old Night, bespoke and without the modularity that would later typify the aesthetic of humanity's ultra-rapid expansion to the stars. Morningstar had been settled early in the golden age of exploration, and Zharrukin was one of its earliest cities.

'Was this where Morningstar's first king raised his capital?' Atharva asked as the dust danced in his hand. 'Why did your world alone stand untouched by the madness, but this city fall? Did your hubris bring you down, your greed? Or was it simply your time? Would that I could talk to you. What might you teach me?'

Atharva knew he was being overly sentimental, but the thought of knowledge being forgotten was as painful to him as a gunshot. He eased his mind into an elevated plane of thought – something the Legion's newly established cults, the Fellowships, were calling 'Enumerations'.

He'd read variants of the technique in the few ancient Achaemenian texts that had survived Cardinal Tang's purge of the Shi-Wu library, but only since leaving Prospero had he begun to perfect the technique. The Enumerations allowed him to focus perfectly on the task at hand, to better construct the mental architecture required to face any given situation.

Atharva studied the play of particles in his palm, watching them spin in ever more complex iterations. Iron oxide particles glittered, the remnants of something ancient and metallic, long since gone to dust amid the ruined city. He sought meaning in the patterns, echoes of the future woven within the random interactions of the dust's gyrations. Future-scrying had always been his focus, but sifting meaning from the Great Ocean's depths had always been challenging.

He glanced from the dancing red dust to the curvature of his left shoulder guard. Emblazoned in pale ivory upon crimson was the serpentine star icon of the Thousand Sons Legion.

Within it was the staring eye of his new Fellowship.

Athanaean.

The name felt new to him, yet spoke of ancient learnings, of a time when wizened academics pored over many quaint and curious volumes of forgotten lore. Atharva was well aware of the mystical significance of names, and this one held a power all its own. The cult's teachings – and those of the Corvidae, the Pavoni and the rest – granted him power he had never dreamed possible. They had allowed him to achieve things all but unknown in the days before Prospero.

Before the Legion's rebirth.

He eased the barriers within his mind, allowing the Great Ocean to seep into his flesh. It flowed into his body like water pouring along a complex series of aqueducts, directed and shaped by the mental thought-forms of the third Enumeration.

He thrilled to the sense of the unknown becoming known, of the unseen and unwritten possibilities now being revealed. A tantalising image formed in his mind, a fleeting glimpse of a dreaming city at the top of the world, its spires molten as the world burned around it.

Was this Zharrukin's doom?

'What are you doing?' asked a muffled voice behind him, and the moment was gone. The flames fell away from his sight and he quelled the build-up of power within him, sighing as the mundane reality of the world reasserted itself.

'Thinking,' he said, opening the fingers of his gauntlet and letting the winds howling through the city blow the dust away.

Atharva wiped the last of it from his palm and turned as he rose to his full height in the centre of the windswept thorough-fare. The crimson of his bulky war-plate reflected the tortured light of the sky, making it shimmer as if with a veneer of oil.

An elegantly proportioned woman with charcoal-black skin stood before him, tightly wrapped in a brightly coloured robe of interlocking geometric patterns. He'd assumed her attire was ceremonial when they'd first met, but he had since learned it was culturally significant, indicating scholarly status within the peoples of the equatorial regions.

Behind her, a Legion Stormbird and two Cervantes-class

transporters sat sheltered from the oncoming storm in the lee of a debris cliff. Their engines thrummed with noise and power, spooling up in readiness for launch.

'Conservator Ashkali,' he said. 'What can I do for you?'

'Niko,' she said. 'I think we've explored these old ruins long enough to dispense with formalities, don't you?'

'As you say,' he replied, both of them knowing he would never refer to her by her first name.

Niko Ashkali was Morningstar's senior conservator: a Terran by birth, but a native at heart. She led the excavations in and around the ruins of Zharrukin, and she had proven to be a thorough and perceptive academic. Her steel-grey hair was bound up in a patterned headscarf and the glare goggles of a rebreather obscured her features.

She pulled up her goggles, revealing startlingly green eyes set in deeply lined sockets. She shielded her gaze from the billowing dust and pointed to the sky.

'We have to evacuate the dig site,' she said, her voice muted by the dust-filter covering her mouth. 'Meterologicus says the magna-storm is at least an hour out, which probably means it'll hit us in ten minutes.'

Atharva lifted his gaze to the mountains in the east. The flaring detonations of a colossal magnetic storm marched over their summits. It was impossible to tell which way the planet's unpredictable weather systems would hurl them.

'The storm front is moving down to sweep across the plains,' he said. 'It will likely pass Zharrukin.'

'Or it could just as easily change course,' replied Ashkali. 'If it hits us, it's going to tear through this place in a blizzard of rogue magnetics and lightning. Anyone still here is going to die.'

Atharva was loath to leave Zharrukin, but to stay would be to risk the lives of the conservator's staff of archaeotechs and all they had unearthed thus far.

'You are correct,' he said. 'Prepare for departure.'

'What of your master? Is he still out there?'

Atharva hesitated before answering.

'He is. Get your people back to their ships.'

Ashkali hesitated before nodding and speaking into her rebreather's integral vox to issue the recall order. Atharva turned and walked back to the Stormbird and did the same, though he sent the order to his warriors via telepathic pulse. Within forty-five seconds, legionaries in crimson war-plate emerged from various areas of the ruins. Each was trailed by a bulk-servitor hauling the fruits of their excavations.

They boarded the Stormbird without a word, securing their findings in the hold before strapping themselves into the contoured benches along the gunship's inner hull.

Ashkali's people took longer to return, hurrying back to their waiting transports with barely disguised panic. The storm was getting worse, the sky flickering with radioactive sunspots and boiling atmospheric superstorms.

In the face of the worsening conditions, the conservator directed the evacuation with clipped efficiency, ensuring everything they had discovered was inventoried on her bronzed data-slate.

Phosis T'kar was the last to board, and the lieutenant paused as he reached Atharva. Dust caked the grooves of his armour and his aura was bellicose, his mind that of a scholar who attacks a work with brute-force reasoning. His methodology wasn't pretty, but it got results.

'Where is he?' he asked.

'He is not here,' replied Atharva, watching the storm descend on the far reaches of Zharrukin.

'That's not what I asked.'

'I know.'

'He should be here.'

'Yes, indeed he should.'

'Then where is he?'

Atharva did not answer, lifting his gaze to the mountains as the storm struck the earth beyond the edge of the city. Raging plumes of lightning-shot dust and debris were hurled hundreds of metres into the air, arcing over the city. A mushroom cloud of fire erupted from its shattered outskirts. Another swiftly followed, rubble lifted high by twisting currents of air and torsioning magnetics. A harsh, metallic-tasting wind blew hard from the mountains, making the mechanics of his war-plate hum in protest.

'We should be in the air,' said Phosis T'kar.

'He will be here. And if he is not, this storm will not trouble him.'

'You can't know that. What do any of us really know about him? What he can do or what he can endure? We barely know him.'

Atharva did not answer. That Phosis T'kar was right made him only more reluctant to admit to his ignorance. The Stormbird vibrated with potential, the pilot keeping it on the ground with a light touch, ready to lift off in an instant.

'Give the order,' said Phosis T'kar.

'Not yet.'

The tallest spires of Zharrukin swayed and groaned, the reinforcement within the stone tearing as alternating fields of powerful magnetics twisted them. Stone and steel peeled from buildings and spun away into the storm as searing winds buffeted the gunship. Dust raged within the Stormbird's troop compartment, swirling in vortices of geomantic significance.

The vox-bead in his helmet chirruped: an incoming message from Mistress Ashkali.

'Master Atharva! We must take off. Right now!'

He nodded and said, 'Go. Get out of here. We will be right behind you.'

'See that you are!'

The two Cervantes-class transports lifted into the air on plumes of jetfire, swaying and lurching wildly, as if the storm winds actively sought to prevent their escape. The first craft took off in the lee of a shattered structure that sheltered it from the worst of the winds. The pilot feathered the engines and Atharva lost sight of it as rusted-ochre clouds closed in.

The second craft was not so lucky.

It twisted as a magnetic squall pulled its starboard wing down and buckled the metal of its hull. Ultra-rapid polarity shifts swung it around like a leaf in a hurricane. It flipped over onto its side, hurtling towards the ground and certain destruction.

Atharva slammed his mind into the second Enumeration.

Raw kine energy flowed through him.

He gripped the faltering transport with his power.

+Help me!+ he cried, the words blurted in a psychic shout.

Phosis T'kar was at his side an instant later, hands extended as he too unleashed his power. Atharva's lieutenant was a practitioner of the kinetic arts, and his sigil of the Raptora cult glittered in the flickering lightning.

Together they halted the transport's tumbling fall.

Atharva and Phosis T'kar rolled their wrists in perfect concert, moulding the kine power to their will. The transport mimicked their movements, rotating like a designer's schematic being haptically manipulated. Its engines flared as the pilot fed every scrap of power to them.

+Release!+ said Atharva.

He and Phosis T'kar relinquished their hold on the transport.

It shot skywards like a stone from a sling.

Bone-deep repercussive pain surged through Atharva's flesh, pain he would endure tenfold later. He let out a charged breath and stepped from the Stormbird's ramp. He read Phosis T'kar's confusion.

'What are you doing?' asked his lieutenant. 'Get back on board.'

'Return to Calaena immediately,' replied Atharva through bloodied teeth. 'Assist the Fourth Legion elements in the evacuation. I will rejoin you when I can.'

Phosis T'kar shook his head and pressed his palm against the closing mechanism. 'I'm closing up, but we aren't leaving without you and the primarch.'

Atharva saw the determination in Phosis T'kar's aura and knew that any argument he might make against this course of action would be futile.

'Then I will attempt to be quick,' he said.

Hurricanes of abrasive dust flensed the paint from his armour in silver streaks as he turned towards the city where his master awaited.

If he is still alive.

Could any being survive conditions so inimical to life?

The clouds parted and a towering figure wreathed in multi-coloured fire emerged from the storm in answer.

He was a giant in crimson and gold, a warrior and scholar in one. His golden war-plate had been crafted by the finest armourers of Terra, a masterpiece of curling horns, sculpted muscles, carved lions and the finest scriptwork. A kilt of leather hung to his knees, and a hook-bladed sword crafted from Prosperine silksteel was belted at his waist next to a colossal tome of psychic lore.

+My lord,+ said Atharva, using his psychic voice.

Magnus the Red was wrought from wrath and wonder, his face a protean blend of features that Atharva had never been able to entirely fix in his mind. A disconcerting attribute in a leader, one that would take some getting used to.

Atharva wasn't sure he was there yet.

The psychic fire of the primarch's magnificent aura kept the storm's fury at bay. Magnus might have been strolling through

Tizca's sculpture gardens, for all the tempest affected him. A trio of servitors followed him, each hauling a high-sided grav-sled.

+Cutting it a bit close, are you not?+ said Atharva.

The primarch looked up, as if he hadn't noticed the storm at all.

+I had not completed my work,+ replied Magnus.

Zharrukin fought to keep the Stormbird from escaping.

Magnetic vortices shredded its belly and spiteful winds hammered the fuselage with flying debris. The gunship's engines burned blue-hot and its superstructure shrieked as if it were being torn apart.

Atharva felt the ground fall away with a sickening lurch. His head slammed against a stanchion as the storm sought to crush them. The pilot fought with all his skill, but against some foes, there could be no victory.

Blitzing winds howled into the Stormbird as a portion of the fuselage peeled away like foil. Sparks and explosions cascaded down the length of the gunship as rogue electromagnetic bursts fried circuitry and the control mechanisms worked into its structure.

+We're losing power to the engines!+

Shredded metal ripped from the side of the gunship as its nose dropped back to the ground. Phosis T'kar threw a kine shield over the breach and the noise of the wind fell away. The Stormbird heeled over, spun on its central axis, and Atharva watched the splintering ruins of Zharrukin racing up to meet them. Magnetic squalls ripped ancient buildings from their foundations and hurled them against one another like a child smashing toy bricks together.

Then, an instant from impact, the gunship levelled out.

The same kaleidoscopic fire that wreathed Magnus as he walked from the ruins burned beyond the breach.

Atharva tore his gaze from the storm's inferno below to where Magnus stood at the prow of the gunship, one hand on his great book of lore. His aura blazed with a brilliant light, too radiant to look upon directly. It filled the interior of the gunship, a power of such magnitude that it made his own seem paltry.

That their new leader was a master of the psychic arts had been obvious the moment Atharva had set eyes upon him.

But this was exceptional.

'Take us home, pilot,' said Magnus.

The Stormbird swiftly caught up to the lumbering Cervantes transports, and the pilot eased back on its thrust. Atharva sensed the gunship's unwillingness to slow, its hunter's name and hunter's heart reluctant to linger with such ungainly flyers.

The fire beyond the breached fuselage faded as the gunship flew beyond the storm's reach, but Phosis T'kar maintained the kine shield all the way to the planetary capital of Calaena.

The gunship circled the city, awaiting clearance to enter its dangerously overcrowded airspace. While Magnus spoke to the pilot, Atharva studied the city below as a man might study an overcrowded ant-farm.

Calaena was a thriving trade hub built at the termination of the arrow-straight river valley that had its origins beyond Zharrukin. Here, the valley widened to form a vast bowl enclosed by high cliffs on three sides and by a bottle-green ocean on the fourth. Calaena's buildings were older than any other Atharva had seen in his travels from Terra: glorious, domed basilicas, rotating towers of phototropic glass, grand libraries and bustling commercial districts that welcomed vessels from off-world and ocean-going haulers from all across Morningstar.

A convoluted web of transit routes, maglevs and curling arterials converged on Calaena from every direction, all monstrously overburdened by incoming traffic. Roadcars were nose to tail and thousands of the planet's inhabitants walked alongside the choked highways, refugees bearing all they owned in the hopes of securing swift passage off-world.

The city itself was normally home to around seventy thousand souls, but with the planetary evacuation in full flow, its population had reached three quarters of a million and was growing larger every day.

The skies of Calaena resembled an insect hive responding to an attack. Swarms of aircraft circled the outskirts of the city, a thousand more rising on intricately plotted flight paths from Vashti Eshkol's control tower on the edge of its offshore starport.

Every ship capable of trans-orbital flight had been pressed into service ferrying Morningstar's population ships anchored in low orbit. Agri-barques now carried people instead of vats of protein gruel and gene-crops, while the stalls of livestock haulers were packed with men and women being taken to life rather than the slaughterman's maul.

Accidents were far from uncommon, with desperate pilots racing into the sky in defiance of Vashti's orders. Most times they were quickly redirected with electromagnetic tethers or – in the case of one unsanctioned launch – shot down over the ocean by the starport's defence turrets to prevent a lethal cascade effect of collisions and crashes.

At the centre of the starport was the *Lux Ferem*, a titanic mass-conveyor from a bygone age of space exploration, when it was expected that these star-faring leviathans would land and become part of a newly colonised planet's infrastructure. Lost arts of technology had powered supremely powerful repulsor generators worked into its thousand-metre hull, allowing a vessel that ought not to have been able to survive atmospheric breach to land and return to the stars.

Its vast bulk vented heat as provosts and legionaries directed frightened civilians onto its embarkation ramps: sixty thousand already, and fifty thousand more yet to board.

Newly constructed towers on the cliffs that enclosed the city were minimising the impact of rogue magnetics in the local area, but not even the technical genius of their construction could keep the area entirely stable. Each was a glaring eyesore, thought Atharva, a boxy, riveted thing of bare girders and yellow-and-black hazard stripes.

The architects of these towers had made planetfall barely a month after the arrival of the Thousand Sons, but they had already made an indelible mark on Morningstar. The entirety of the westernmost cliff had been sculpted into a basalt-black citadel known as the Sharei Maveth, its full height reshaped into an impregnable bulwark, the rock within blasted, cut and burned into defensive galleries, wide parapets, firing steps and macro-cannon emplacements.

It was towards this grim stronghold that the Stormbird angled its prow as its final approval to approach was granted – a narrow flight path threading the absurdly overcrowded skies. To deviate from the prescribed manoeuvres even a fraction would almost certainly result in a mid-air collision.

Atharva craned his neck to study the Sharei Maveth as the gunship dropped down through the morass of aircraft. Its construction was mathematically precise and yet was not without a proud, martial beauty. Its towers were finished with decorative finials, its gun ports worked with functionless embellishments and its gates carved with frescoes that spoke of an artist's mind shackled by practicality.

'My brother does so like to make a statement,' said Magnus, returning to the crew compartment.

Atharva found the notion that his gene-sire had a single brother, let alone that he was now one of *twelve*, hard to comprehend. That an individual so singular counted so many others like him seemed absurd, as though a pantheon of demigods had chosen to abandon their divine abode and play a part in the affairs of mortals.

Atharva had seen none of his father's brothers, but he had heard tell of their deeds. The legends of the primarchs were already spreading throughout the crusading fleets: tales of impossible odds overcome and heroic achievements that Atharva might have dismissed as garishly hyperbolic.

But having seen his own primarch in action, he knew better.

'He did all this in a single day?' asked Atharva.

'He did,' confirmed Magnus. 'Of course, given a free hand, we could achieve far greater in a fraction of the time.'

'We could?'

'Of course,' said Magnus, giving him a curious look.

The Stormbird twisted on its axis over one of the upper landing platforms, and Atharva heard the whine of its landing claws deploying. Surrounding turrets followed the gunship's motion, and Atharva frowned at the bellicose intent he sensed within every one of them.

The Stormbird groaned as the pilot set it down and the wounded superstructure eased. The pitch of the engines rose as the pilot cut power. Atharva let out a relieved breath.

The Thousand Sons unharnessed and began disembarkation preparations as the frontal assault ramp lowered with a grating whine of protesting mechanisms.

'Walk with me, Atharva,' said Magnus, 'and meet my brother of Olympus.'

Only later would Atharva be able to clearly recall his first meeting with Perturabo of the Iron Warriors.

Rain began to fall as he stepped from the belly of the injured Stormbird – hard, slashing rain that bounced from his armour and washed the dust of Zharrukin from its plates. Glaring stab-lights from a covering firestep swept the platform, catching every droplet, which seemed to be falling in slow motion.

Four figures emerged from the fortress and advanced through the rain. Three were legionaries in burnished plates of hulking iron rendered slate-grey in the shadows of their surroundings. They advanced shoulder to shoulder, and each bore a curved, rectangular shield upon his left side, with a sheathed gladius held fast upon his right.

Leading them was Perturabo of Olympus.

Atharva's step faltered at the sight of the Lord of Iron.

The primarch was a giant whose likeness might have been carved from the same rock as the mountains. Jutting over his wide shoulder plates was the wire-wound grip of an enormous broadsword worthy of the ancient war gods. Suddenly, tales of Perturabo felling entire armies with a single blow seemed not so far-fetched.

Clad in titanic plates of Terminator armour, he towered over his warriors, his strength vast and depthless like an approaching thunderhead. His power was brutally direct, yet it was without arrogance, leavened with open features that broke into a ready smile at the sight of Magnus.

'The Meterologicus feared you taken by the magna-storm,' said Perturabo, his words beaten upon the air like forge hammers on hot metal. 'But I told them it would take more than a city-killing storm to bring down Magnus the Red.'

'Had we waited a minute longer before abandoning Zharrukin, they would have been right,' said Magnus. 'But what I learned in that final minute may make all the difference, brother.'

The primarchs embraced, like armoured beasts seeking to assert dominance over a rival. They came apart and Atharva saw no rivalry, only shared brotherhood.

Brother. That word again...

The primarchs were so different in aspect and power, so diametrically opposed it seemed lunacy to imagine them springing from the same genetic root. But to look deeper was to see a shared passion for artistry and hidden knowledge, a love of beauty and the art of rendering wonders.

Atharva's eyes roamed Perturabo's armour, taking in every curve and line, every flourish of a master craftsman, together with the many modifications that bore the hallmarks of one whose knowledge of machinery was unmatched. In a moment of revelation, Atharva understood that the primarch himself had made these alterations.

Perturabo spoke again, but Atharva was not listening. It took him a moment to realise that the words were not for Magnus, but for him.

'My lord?' he said.

'My armour,' Perturabo repeated. 'Is there something awry with its construction?'

'No, my lord,' said Atharva, finding it suddenly hard to form the right words as the primarch's stare bored into him like a drill. 'I... I was just admiring its workmanship. The embellishments are... quite unique.'

'Tell me what you see,' commanded Perturabo.

Atharva's mouth was suddenly dry, and he took a moment to gather his thoughts before speaking.

'I see the handiwork of Terrawatt armourers, pre-Unity designs and eastern skill,' he said, trying not to let the primarch's appraising gaze distract him. 'I see distant echoes of Narodnyan craft, but echoes nonetheless. The baroque turns on the plastron and gorget lead me to believe these plates were wrought in the Kholat Syakhl forges.'

'You have a good eye, Atharva,' said Perturabo, and Atharva was humbled the primarch knew his name. 'What else?'

He looked closer, now seeing the curling script winding around the edges of the primarch's gauntlets, breastplate, greaves and pauldrons. They were not, as he had first thought, discrete armourers' marks, but a single inscription moving from piece to piece.

'You bear a nomenclature sequence,' said Atharva. 'Similar to that of the Emperor's Custodians, but I do not recognise the language.'

'It is Ur-Phoenician,' said Perturabo. 'One of the earliest languages known to humankind. This is a variant argot carried from Old Earth to become the first language of Olympia.'

'What does it say?'

'Nothing I wish to share,' said Perturabo, turning once again to Magnus, and Atharva felt a curious mix of relief at a burden being removed from his shoulders and regret that he could not bear it a little longer. 'So, brother, did you find anything in those ruins worth the price you almost paid?'

'Time will tell,' said Magnus, as Thousand Sons legionaries began the process of unloading the Stormbird. Already XV Legion Techmarines and Mechanicum adepts were working to repair the damage wrought by the storm. Acetylene sparks and mag-welders flickered at its belly.

Magnus gestured to the grav-sleds of recovered artefacts and said, 'We uncovered sealed archives and found much that predates the Great Crusade by centuries. Any one of them could be the key to revealing why this world alone of all the others in this system survived the cataclysm of Old Night unscathed.'

'Why is that knowledge so important to you?'

'It should be important to all of us,' said Magnus.

'We have more pressing concerns just now.'

Magnus affected a look of mock superiority and said, 'I seem to remember it was you who all but begged me to stay another hour in Boeotia to try and find the Library of Kadmus before the promethium infernos set the mountains ablaze.'

Perturabo smiled at the shared memory.

'We never did find it, did we?'

'No, and not a day goes by where I do not regret denying you that extra hour.'

'Have no regrets on that front,' said Perturabo. 'Mount Cithaeron was ablaze from foothills to summit ten minutes after we left. Had we stayed, we would have died.'

'But we would have died enlightened,' said Magnus.

Perturabo gestured to the aircraft-filled sky.

'We are not here to save knowledge,' said Perturabo. 'We are here to save lives.'

'Both are vital to the future,' said Magnus.

'Aye, there's truth in that,' agreed Perturabo. 'But I wonder which you value higher.'

TWO

REVERSAL • CRIMSON AND IRON • DOOMSAYERS

A planet-wide state of emergency had been declared on Morningstar six Terran standard months previously. The first signs of the impending disaster came when a building atmospheric disturbance suddenly developed into a raging magnetic cyclone that ripped a twelve-thousand-kilometre swathe of devastation across the southern hemisphere.

At first, this storm was believed to be an anomaly, a once-in-a-lifetime tragic occurrence never to be expected again.

Six days later, local defence forces were scrambled to investigate a total failure of power in the belt-hives of the equatorial region. Tens of thousands died as coolant units failed and hydro-recycling facilities ceased functioning.

A weaponised electromagnetic detonation was suspected, and members of an outlawed cult known as the Sons of Shaitan were named as the principal suspects. A relic from the days when men still put their faith in gods and daemons, its tattooed members preached a doomsday doctrine that welcomed this apocalypse as a sign they were soon to sit at the right hand of their golden deity.

But the truth was far worse.

Mechanicum investigations revealed the source of the power failure to be a localised, high-gradient reversal of the magnetic fields generated in Morningstar's core. Fluctuations in a planet's magnetic field were not uncommon, though incidents of such focused strength were virtually unknown.

When three more incidents occurred over the next seven days, enough data was generated by the Mechanicum Geologicus for its adepts to identify the nature of these disasters.

Morningstar was in the midst of an ultra-rapid geomagnetic polarity reversal.

Such events were common to all planets, with the periods between each shift lasting somewhere in the region of half a million years or thereabouts. Reversals in polarity typically took centuries to complete, and were so gradual as to pass all but unnoticed by the planet's inhabitants.

The Mechanicum's best-case scenario put the length of this reversal at six months. What was causing this hyper-accelerated reversal was unknown, but its effects were proving devastating.

Magna-storms ripped through the atmosphere with increasing regularity and ferocity, disrupting power grids all across the planet. For three rotations, every light on Morningstar was snuffed out by a planet-wide electromagnetic hurricane, with only firelight to keep the darkness at bay. A magnetic-static hash of screaming voices disrupted all but the most powerful vox-systems, and riots erupted in a score of cities as food and water distribution ground to a halt.

Violent seismic activity tore the planet's crust open in forking split lines. Morningstar's largest hive conurbation, built straddling a geothermal fissure, had sank into the fiery chasm that once supplied its power needs when the groaning tectonic plate broke apart.

That same earthquake drowned another three coastal cities beneath tsunamis hundreds of metres high.

The planet's population was quartered in a single month.

If such disasters were not bad enough, Mechanicum theorists predicted an ultra-rapid erosion of Morningstar's atmosphere, resulting in lethal exposure levels of stellar radiation.

Faced with the prospect of mass extinction, the Imperial Governor Konrad Vargha finally declared Morningstar lost and broadcast evacuation protocols on every functioning vox.

Only the planetary capital of Calaena retained a functioning starport with the capacity to handle a large-scale evacuation. Within hours of Vargha's broadcast, the planet's populace were making their way to this last refuge to secure passage off-world. They arrived over the next weeks in their hundreds of thousands, and the people of Calaena opened their doors to every one.

And when the city quickly became full, well-planned refugee camps were built in its surrounding environs, sprawling cities of canvas and plasflex shelters.

The port facilities of Calaena were robust and extensive, but it swiftly became clear that Morningstar's fleet assets were woefully ill-equipped and insufficient to effect a mass evacuation.

Appeals for salvation were hurled into the depths of space via dreaming astropaths, desperate pleas for any nearby Expeditionary Fleets to divert and offer their vessels to aid in the evacuation.

A response was received from the XV Legion seventeen hours later. By fortunate happenstance, Magnus and his Thousand Sons were traversing the outer edges of the system and offered their assistance. Barely a decade out from its sabbatical on Prospero, the XV Legion fleet was yet to rebuild its full strength and would itself require additional help to ensure as much of Morningstar's populace was saved as possible.

Fifty-four days later, the IV Legion answered.

* * *

Ahzek Ahriman wished he had seen Calaena in its prime.

The city's architecture was of a style that evoked memories of a world he left decades ago and which he knew he would likely never see again.

He imagined this was what cities at mankind's peak must have been like: graceful, well proportioned, harmonious in their reverence for what had come before and cognisant of the coming future.

A hard rain was blowing in from the ocean, freighted with hot fumes of the thousands of lighters, barques, transits, shuttles and atmosphere lifters ferrying men, women and children to the ships in orbit.

The sky was a furious mix of purple, orange and pink, the churning atmospherics and the sheer mass of metal transforming it into something unpredictable and dangerous. Jetwash and arcing contrails criss-crossed the clouds, together with flashes of lightning and the slow dance of distant spots of light – warships in geostationary low anchor.

The wide, tree-lined street he and his opposite number from the Iron Warriors were marching along was known locally as the Boulevard of Firmaments. Each of its individual cobbles was patterned with a celestial arrangement visible from one of Morningstar's many observatories.

However, none of those cobbles could be seen due to the tens of thousands of frightened rain-soaked people moving miserably along its length en route to the gates of the star port. At hundred-metre intervals, armed legionaries kept the packed crowds of refugees moving and contained. The same scenes were played out every day on every major street of Calaena: Space Marines marching the day's randomly allocated rota of evacuees from the camps set up around the city towards the starport.

Assuming the Mechanicum's estimates of how long Morningstar had left were accurate, Perturabo's genius for logistics would ensure the majority of its people were off-world before the planet's impending doom.

Ahriman knew there had been protests at the heavy-handedness of the primarch's plan, but when the first batches of refugees were lifted into orbit on schedule, most died away.

Most, but not all.

Scattered doomsayers in the golden, lightning-embossed robes of the Sons of Shaitan occasionally hectored refugees from rooftops or makeshift pulpits. Swift action was taken wherever such troublemakers were encountered, yet their message appeared to be gaining traction with a small minority of Morningstar's populace, who began leaving the camps and making their way to the regions of greatest danger in search of lethal rapture.

Yet for all the cult's doomsaying, Ahriman sensed little panic among Morningstar's people.

Uncertainty, yes. Fear, undoubtably, but no panic.

Whatever geological failings Morningstar had as a planet, its people were disciplined citizens of the Imperium and stalwart in the face of adversity. He sensed no psychic potential among the population around him, which was unusual, but not without precedent.

'We need to get them moving faster,' said Ahriman's armoured companion on the other side of the street. His iron yellow-and-black armour glistened in the rain. He spoke over their internal vox, scanning the crowds with a calculating gaze. 'I'm getting word of backlogs and choke points all across the city.'

'These are ordinary people, not livestock, Forrix,' said Ahriman. 'Nor are they legionaries. They do not march as we march. If we goad them to greater speed, we will only turn their fear into full-blown panic. Then people will die.'

Forrix was an Iron Warrior, a Legion Ahriman knew had little patience for mortal foibles. He had fought alongside elements

of the IV twice, but that was in the days before either Legion
had been reunited with its primarch.

For the Thousand Sons, that great day had come thirteen
years ago; it was barely four in the case of the Iron Warriors.

'They should be afraid,' said Forrix. 'Fear is a great motivator.'

'Hope is a better one.'

Ahriman sensed Forrix bite back on a caustic retort.

'You disagree?' said Ahriman.

'I do, but this is not the time for idle banter,' said Forrix. 'My
primarch's timetable allows for no leeway.'

'I believe it is the planet's self-destructive timetable we ought
to be more concerned with,' said Ahriman. 'Can your primarch
plan for that too?' He sensed Forrix bristle at the implied insult
to his gene-sire, and added, 'I meant no insult.'

'Then you should think before you speak,' said Forrix.

'No warrior of the Thousand Sons would do otherwise.'

'Implying that the Fourth does not?'

Ahriman sighed. The IV were a Legion of methodical mind-
sets, quick to find fault in others.

How might the influence of their primarch mitigate that?

'No, Forrix, and if you persist in seeing insults in my every
utterance where none are intended, then this is going to be a
very long day,' said Ahriman, diffusing the choler in the Iron
Warrior's aura with a gentle psychic pressure.

'I apologise, Legionary Ahriman.'

'My name is Ahzek.'

'Kydomor,' said Forrix. 'My name is Kydomor.'

The *Harvest Dawn* lifted from the outermost radial platform
on a trail of dirty jetwash. Her ascent was erratic as she fought
Morningstar's gravity before her engines stabilised and she
hauled her ungainly bulk onto her assigned flight path.

Vashti Eshkol watched the agri-hauler climb into orbit through the armourglass windows of Calaena's orbital command centre, hoping against all reason that the vessel's primitive drive units would get her into orbit. Vashti had grounded the *Harvest Dawn* for a mandatory refit seven months ago, but Primarch Perturabo's evacuation plan demanded every vessel – no matter how dilapidated – be pressed into service.

Skitarii forager cohorts were combing every breaker yard, silo and hive sump within six hundred kilometres for anything that might manage even one trip into space.

'I detect elevated adrenal levels in your bloodstream, commander,' said Magos Tessza Rom, speaking from the centre of the chamber.

'Are you surprised?' asked Vashti, making her way back to her own command station, a simple brass-faced console inset with numerous data-slates. From here she could interface directly with each departing ship's avionics, direct the starport's defence guns and observe the intricate ballet of departures.

'Not even a little,' said Rom. 'Every launch sees your adrenaline levels spike. It is a classic fight-or-flight response – significant hormonal cascade, increased blood pressure and heightened levels of neurotransmitters.'

'Fight or flight? I know which I'd rather do,' said Vashti, watching the *Harvest Dawn*'s trajectory as it passed from the troposphere to the stratosphere. In around sixty seconds, it would be someone else's responsibility.

'Fight,' said Rom, and Vashti grinned.

'Always,' she said. 'But for now, I think I need something to take the edge off a little.'

Vashti pressed her hand to the skin at her collarbone, haptic implants beneath her fingertips activating the implanted reservoir of bio-stabilisers. She blinked at the sudden clarity of her vision and felt her pulse steady.

'And now you are calm again,' said Rom. 'Good.'

Rom's station was elevated behind hers, the Mechanicum adept's chimeric form suspended in a full-body harness at the centre of a sphere of noospheric data streams. Ocular-neural implants allowed Vashti to perceive what Rom was seeing, and she winced every time she saw how dangerously overcrowded her airspace had become.

Her thirty-strong staff of techs and servitors were strung out and exhausted from coordinating the enormous volume of traffic from ground to orbit. Most were working on stimms and would suffer terrible withdrawals when the evacuation was done. Some might not even survive, but not one had complained at the daunting task before them.

She quickly identified the *Harvest Dawn*'s track, a steady climb towards the low anchors of the Iron Warriors fleet lines. Barring something catastrophic, the agri-hauler would soon be unloading its eight thousand passengers.

'The *Dawn* is more than six centuries old,' said Vashti. 'She's a rust-bucket that ought to have been mothballed decades ago. It's only hope and blind faith that keeps her aloft.'

'The *Harvest Dawn* is well past its allotted service years,' agreed Rom, 'but such tolerances must be waived in the face of current circumstances.'

'She's made twelve round trips already, and we're pushing our luck asking her to make a thirteenth.'

'Is that superstition?' said Rom.

'Common sense,' answered Vashti.

'It is much the same thing.'

'Is that humour?'

'Experience,' said Rom.

'Circuit hub Epsilon-Five-Alpha requesting hand-off,' said Rom as the *Harvest Dawn*'s orbital track flashed amber.

'I see it. Authorisation granted. Let them have her.'

'Preparing to hand off to orbital controllers aboard the *Iron Blood*,' said Rom. 'In five, four, three, two, one. Mark.'

The flashing amber track changed to a solid blue.

'Another one away!' cried Korinna Moreno, one of Vashti's senior orbital controllers. She punched the air, revealing a porcelain-smooth augmetic arm painted with coiling serpents, and a hoarse cheer went up from the command centre staff.

'What's next on the slate?' asked Vashti.

'*The Gallant* and the *Vos Shermentov*,' replied Moreno, bringing up a pair of wireframe hololiths and technical specifications. 'A pair of dirty promethium rigs that limped clear of the equatorial magna-storm.'

'Promethium rigs. Wonderful,' sighed Vashti. 'I'm sure they'll be *totally* safe to launch.'

Ahriman and Forrix passed into the grand processionals of the western districts en route to the starport. Vapour pillars of departing vessels columned the volatile sky and a nimbus of flickering energy hazed the air above the cliff-like dorsal surfaces of the *Lux Ferem*.

Rain was still falling in an ionised flood, and Ahriman felt a momentary flicker of prescience, seeing another storm-wracked city lashed by rain in its final moments.

With names exchanged, a bridge of sorts had been established between Ahriman and Forrix, and they spoke now with the halting cadences of men who might yet be brothers.

'Were you born on Olympia?' asked Ahriman as they passed beneath a polished ouslite arch commemorating the arrival of the Crusade fleets in Morningstar's system.

'No, I am one of the few remaining Iron Warriors to have been born on Terra,' said Forrix. 'I spent my boyhood in the shadow of the great mountain of Eite Mòhr, but my heart is Olympian. As soon as I set foot on its rocky uplands, I knew I was home.'

'What is it like?'

'Ah, how can I describe our home?' said Forrix, fond memories rendering his aura a warm honeyed colour. 'It is a world to lift the soul, Ahzek. Endless mountains of dark beauty and sweet-smelling stands of highland fir as far as the eye can see.'

'It sounds magnificent,' said Ahriman.

'It is,' agreed Forrix. 'But it is not a world to take lightly either. Olympia is a harsh and testing world, a world that is not kind to the weak. The black rock of the mountains is hard and unforgiving, and it does it yield easily to pick or hammer. But prove your mettle and you will know what it is to be a worthy man. Yet even as Olympia lifts you, it reminds you of your place in the universe.'

'How so?' said Ahriman, feeling a flutter of discord somewhere within the trudging crowds. The sensation was fleeting, for the people of Morningstar had minds blunted to psychic probing. Ahriman eased his consciousness into Corvidae thought-forms, hoping to catch a stray future-echo.

'The mountains of Olympia have existed for millions of years and they will exist for millions more,' said Forrix. 'No matter the affairs of men, their struggles and their triumphs, the mountains will endure. To know that makes a man humble, for he will be long gone before the mountains are dust.'

Ahriman was surprised by the poetry of Forrix's words, having not suspected the Iron Warriors of having much of an appreciation of life's transient nature.

'I should like to see Olympia someday,' he said.

'You should. It would do you good to feel humility.'

'Are you suggesting I am arrogant?'

Forrix laughed, the sound like metal grinding on metal. Ahriman sensed Forrix did not laugh much.

'Can any of us say we are not? But you Thousand Sons hold yourselves above all others as scholars and visionaries, warriors who put a greater price on knowledge than all else.'

'You say that like we are to be viewed with suspicion for qualities most would consider a virtue,' Ahriman pointed out.

Forrix shrugged.

'I do not say this to anger you, Ahzek. Only to point out that any man who ascends to the ranks of the Legiones Astartes needs to be humbled every now and then. We transhumans are like gods unto mortals, but we all need a little humility to remind us of the purpose for which we were wrought by the Emperor, beloved by all.'

Anger touched Ahriman, and he sought to quell it by rising into the first Enumeration. Forrix had pleased Ahriman with his insight, so he had no right to be angry with him for speaking honestly.

'You are right, my friend,' he said. 'The Thousand Sons *are* sometimes guilty of hubris, for we are seekers after truth and such a quest sometimes requires us to set ourselves apart from our brothers.'

'Nothing should set a man apart from his brothers,' said Forrix. 'That is surely the greatest truth, but I see my words have angered you, and that was not my intention. Accept my apology and we will talk of your world, yes? I wish to hear of Prospero.'

Ahriman's humours were still unbalanced, but it was not the bilious fire of choler that came to the fore, but the black confusion of melancholia.

'Prospero is a place of… mixed emotion for me,' said Ahriman, startling himself with his need for honesty. 'When we first came to our primarch's home world it was as a broken Legion. I remember it imperfectly, but what I *do* remember is that we were dying.'

'Dying?' said Forrix, genuinely shocked.

'Yes. A… a sickness of a sort had taken hold of us. I think it almost destroyed us.'

'This is why there are so few of you?'

'Yes. The Emperor led us to Prospero, where we were reunited with our primarch, but in truth I remember little of that meeting or much of what happened in its aftermath.'

'Aye, it is said that men in the presence of the Emperor find their memories afflicted,' said Forrix.

That was not what Ahriman meant, but he did not correct the Iron Warrior. Slick sweat like a layer of frost sheened his skin at the memory of the agonies he had been enduring at that moment, every fibre of his being directed at holding back the horror of something so terrible he dared not name it.

'All I remember is Magnus the Red taking a knee and swearing an oath before his father. It was a glorious time for us, a time of rebirth, but I barely recall the months following that meeting.'

'I felt the same thing,' said Forrix. 'We met the Lord of Iron in the rain. Rain just like this. Dammekos presented his adoptive son to his true father atop the Blinded Citadel. What was your primarch's oath?'

'*That* I remember,' said Ahriman, pleased to be asked a question he could answer without a vague feeling of unease or the notion he was revealing his Legion's secrets. 'I shall never forget it. Magnus said, "As I am your son, they shall become mine." Then he took the Emperor's hand to accept primacy of our Legion. That was the moment we *truly* became the Thousand Sons.'

'But tell me of your world, Ahzek,' said Forrix. 'Speak of Prospero's heart, the soul that lives in its stone.'

'My world is Terra, and in truth I saw little of Prospero's landscape. Our Legion was rebuilding its ranks, learning our true potential from our father and welcoming back to the ranks many we thought lost to us. These were heady days, you understand. Our Legion was on the verge of extinction, but Magnus had saved us. We were reborn and our lives given fresh purpose...'

Ahriman's words trailed off as he sensed a flare of emotion in the crowd once more. Forrix immediately saw the change in him and he brought his weapon up.

'What is it? What do you see?'

'Nothing, I see nothing.'

'Your posture says otherwise.'

Ahriman looked down and saw he had drawn his weapon without conscious thought. A bolt was chambered, his finger curled around the trigger and ready to fire. His Corvidae senses were afire, and he traced the glittering lines he saw in his mind back from a moment where he might pull that trigger.

'There!' said Forrix, and Ahriman looked up to see a man break from the crowd to clamber up a statue depicting Damjan Torun, Morningstar's first Light King. He climbed onto the statue's plinth and threw off his stormcloak to reveal an ochre robe threaded with images of golden snakes.

Ahriman recognised the symbol of the Sons of Shaitan.

'Glory of rapture be upon you all!' screamed the man, one hand holding on to the statue's leg, the other raised in a fist. 'The time of our ascension is upon us! We are the blessed ones. We are the chosen people who can choose to rise to join the Stormlord! His tempests shake the heavens, His return splits the land! Can you not feel Him?'

Few among the crowd paid him any heed, but Ahriman sensed more minds than he would have expected responding to the zealot's words.

'Our world missed its chance once, when a lightless age of strife descended upon the galaxy and raised others to His golden palace among the stars! But the Stormlord is nothing if not merciful, and He bestows His wonder of strife upon us again! He offers us this chance to be with Him! We were denied the chance in the rapture of Old Night, but the Sons of Shaitan beseech you now – look to the skies and see the signs of His coming! Welcome them and embrace this golden apocalypse!'

Ahriman pushed into the crowded street, anxious to shut the demagogue down before his words created panic.

'I can end this with a headshot,' said Forrix, shouldering his bolter. Ahriman heard the click of a target link and knew Forrix would not miss.

'No,' he said. 'I'll stop him.'

He drew in a breath of power, feeling the energies of the Great Ocean suffuse his flesh. It touched none of those around him as they fled before his swift advance. Some were jeering at the man, attempting to drown out his doomsaying, but many more were, in turn, heckling those trying to shout him down.

The man saw Ahriman and Forrix advancing towards his perch upon the statue's plinth and jabbed an accusing finger at them.

'Look! The warriors of crimson and iron have come to our world to steal this moment from us, to deny us our rightful place at His side. They herd us like cattle into the vaults of ships to take us from our homes. Do you know where they are taking you? Will they tell us? No! They claim they are our protectors, but I tell you they are daemons given human faces! They are traitors who walk in the darkness between the stars come to enslave us!'

Ahriman extended his will and closed the man's throat with the merest nudge of kine force. The man's words were silenced, and his eyes bulged as he fought to draw breath. Ahriman could have killed him, but he had no wish to murder the man, just deprive him of oxygen long enough to render him unconscious.

But the raving demagogue was not to be denied his martyrdom, and he pulled a snub-nosed autopistol from beneath his robes and placed it to his forehead.

'No!' shouted Ahriman, but even transhuman reflexes could not stop what happened next.

The man pulled the trigger and blasted his brains out onto the watching refugees.

At the man's death, a host of people in the crowd threw off concealing cloaks to reveal serpent-stitched robes identical to the dead man's.

Ahriman saw stubbers, auto-rifles, swords and hatchets.

The Sons of Shaitan fell upon the refugees in a frenzy of gun-fire and slashing blades.

THREE

LET THEM DIE • AHZEK UNBOUND • CRUELTY

Hathor Maat was well aware of the lesser mental capacity of mortals, but this was beyond the pale. The old man before him was trembling in fear, holding himself upright with a wooden staff carved in the form of an elongated viper. Despite his physical frailty, he looked up at Hathor Maat with a defiance that was quite out of character in those facing transhumans.

His name was Felix Tephra and he was the elected spokesman for this horticultural collective on the fertile slopes of Mount Kailash.

Dormant for millennia, Morningstar's geomagnetic upheaval had transformed the serene mountain into a rumbling powder keg on the verge of a catastrophic eruption.

Tephra stood before his people – some five hundred agri-labourers and techs who were ignoring all sense and reason by refusing to be airlifted to safety in the Stormbirds of the Thousand Sons and Iron Warriors.

The isolated community was little more than a score of simple portal-framed structures with corrugated roofs. It possessed only the bare minimum of technology required to operate the irrigation systems and nutrient atomisers of its stepped fields. A winding rail-track led back down the mountain, but Hathor Maat didn't think it had been used in years.

He tapped the Legion insignia upon his shoulder guard with his gauntlet.

'I have been tasked with bringing you to safety,' he said.

'And we thank you,' said Tephra. 'But your efforts were unnecessary. We are–'

Tephra's words were cut off by a hacking, coughing fit. He bent double and would have collapsed but for his staff. When he straightened and took his hand from his mouth, it was wet with black phlegm.

Hathor Maat eased a measure of his psychic senses outwards, his perception of the man's biology superior to any narthecium. Tephra's lungs were all but dissolved by months of breathing pyroclastic ash from the volcano's smouldering peak.

Reaching out to place a hand upon Tephra's shoulder, Hathor Maat let his power – his Pavoni power – flow into the man's flesh. It threaded damaged blood vessels all the way into his chest, where it renewed damaged bronchioles and purged the lung tissue of toxic materials.

Tephra's breathing eased almost instantly, and he looked up at the legionary in wonderment.

'Come back with us and you can all be healed,' said Hathor Maat.

Tephra's wonderment fled his face and he took a step back.

Hathor Maat had seen that look before, in the eyes of enemies trying to kill him. Surely this man would not be so stupid as to attempt something so obviously suicidal?

'Cease your temptations!' hissed Tephra, his fists clenched in anger. 'Leave our sacred mountain. Right now.'

His voice quavered, rich with a giddy elation, as if he had passed some sort of test by spitting in the face of Hathor

Maat's gift, as though dying here was the culmination of some long-awaited fulfilment.

'You *are* aware of Magos Tancorix's readings, yes?' said Hathor Maat, attempting another tack. He held out the slate upon which the Mechanicum's data indicating Mount Kailash's inevitable fate was clearly displayed. 'This volcano is going explode. Not just erupt and pour molten lava down its flanks, but *explode*. This mountain is going to *cease to exist*.'

He was careful to enunciate every syllable, lest there be any misunderstanding. 'My men and I have orders to bring you and your people to Calaena for immediate evacuation.'

Tephra shook his head. 'We are staying. That is an end to the matter.'

Hathor Maat let his awareness spread throughout the men and women gathered behind Tephra. He felt their determination to remain here, a blind righteousness impervious to anything so trivial as facts or reason.

'You're all going to die,' said Hathor Maat, struggling to contain his anger in the face of such wilful stupidity. 'Is that what you want?'

'It is not about what *we* want,' said Tephra. 'It is the will of the Stormlord. We will soon stand in radiance at His side.'

The man's foolishness beggared belief.

Hathor Maat laughed in his face. 'The Stormlord? Do you realise how ridiculous that sounds? You are willing to die and consign everyone here to death over a *folktale?*'

'You dare insult our faith?' said Tephra.

'When your faith is ridiculous, risks the lives of my men and will get everyone here killed, absolutely.'

'Then we have nothing further to talk about,' said Tephra, turning and rejoining his people. Hathor Maat watched, incredulous, as they made their way to their dirt-encrusted homes.

He sighed, his anger turning to resignation, and turned back to the waiting Stormbirds, two in the crimson livery of the Thousand Sons and five in the steeldust yellow-and-black of the Iron Warriors.

Obax Zakayo marched out to meet him.

'What is happening?' asked the Iron Warrior. 'Why are they not boarding the gunships?'

Hathor Maat climbed the assault ramp of his Stormbird.

'They are not coming,' he said.

'What? Why not?'

'They don't want our help. They want to stay.'

Hathor Maat felt Obax Zakayo's confusion discolour his aura. The Iron Warrior did not have the imagination to comprehend such illogical behaviour. Truth be told, Hathor Maat was little better equipped to understand it.

'Ignorance is nothing to be ashamed of,' he said. 'It can be undone by learning, but deliberate stupidity irritates me.'

Hathor Maat looked to the mountaintop. Boiling clouds of ash and lightning raged around the summit; bands of purples, pinks and sick yellow smeared across the buckling sky. His scrying powers were weak in comparison to his new-found potency in biomancy, but Hathor Maat needed no seersight to know that the volcano would soon obliterate every living thing within hundreds of kilometres.

'They will all die here,' said Obax Zakayo.

'Yes, they will.'

'So what are we to do?'

'We let them,' snapped Hathor Maat.

The street was full of screams.

Bodies lay at awkward angles. The ground was slick with blood. Men and women ran from their attackers, but bullets and blades met them at every turn. Husbands sheltered wives and mothers sheltered children. The Sons of Shaitan showed no mercy, turning their weapons on the young and the old, the strong and the weak.

Ahriman's first shot all but obliterated a man carrying a weapon with a long, perforated barrel. The man had killed at least a dozen people with indiscriminate fire, chanting a heathen catechism with each pull of the trigger. His body came apart, blown open by the explosive power of Ahriman's mass-reactive bolt shells. His second shot ripped through three men in a welter of shattered bone and pulped organs.

The deafening echoes of bolter fire overshadowed all other sounds, and every head turned at the deafening reports. People threw themselves to the ground, crawling behind what little cover the streetscape offered.

The gold-robed killers turned their guns on the two legionaries. Bullets sparked from their armour, but such low-powered weapons could do little more than scratch the paint from their plates.

A bolt shell detonated, and another gunman was ripped apart from the inside. Ahriman saw mercury-bright haloes of zeal and certitude surrounding the murderous men and women. His seersight was better than any reticule on his helm visor. His targets were picked out unmistakably.

He fired twice more, killing another two attackers.

Forrix matched his movements, advancing at his right shoulder. He fired with the metronomic regularity of a forge hammer, putting foes down with every shot. They waded through screaming refugees, twin giants with fire spitting from their weapons.

A man wearing a bloodstained fright-mask rose to his knees. A ricocheting fragment had ripped away most of the right side of his torso, leaving him hideously misshapen. He screamed as he fired a blitzing stream of high-calibre shells. They burst into flame an instant before impact as Ahriman surrounded himself and Forrix with a layer of superheated air.

He extended his Pyrae thought-form and hurled the man backwards, his golden robes ablaze. His screams were abruptly cut off as searing fires dragged the oxygen from his lungs and consumed his flesh with phosphex speed.

He felt surprise flow from Forrix, but spun around as his Corvidae senses flickered with a jagged vision of the statue upon which the demagogue had hectored the refugees.

There! Two masked men in golden robes, with an Imperial Army-issue rocket launcher primed and ready to fire. He yelled a warning as the gunner pressed the launch trigger.

The rocket streaked towards Forrix.

The Iron Warrior saw it coming. He braced and bent into the incoming ordnance with a defiant roar.

The warhead impacted dead centre on his shoulder guard, exploding on impact with a percussive hammer blow. Ahriman threw an enclosing kine barrier around Forrix. A storm of razored fragments engulfed the Iron Warrior, but remained trapped within Ahriman's psychic shield.

The two men bent to reload their weapon with a speed that spoke of professional training, but they had already taken the best shot they were ever going to get. Ahriman pushed his thoughts into the eighth Enumeration, the most warlike posture of his Fellowship, and poured his psychic power into their mortal physiology.

They screamed, clawing the flesh from their bones as superheated blood aerosolised from every pore in a stinking red mist. Skin slid like melted wax, bones bent and snapped.

Ahriman let the power of the Great Ocean bleed out, exhaling as his combat instincts sought fresh threats. He registered no more gunfire or screams of terror; weeping and pain were all that remained.

He blinked away freeze-frame after-images of half-remembered truths, a corollary to such reckless expenditure of power.

A brother lost to a terrible curse.

A pain so great his mind fled from its memory.

A great and terrible god reaching deep inside him to push the horror down into the deepest vault within his mind.

Memories close to the surface and yet so far out of reach.

Repercussive pain settled in his marrow and confusion shrouded Ahriman's thoughts. His mind rebelled at being forced to bear such a burden.

A scorched gauntlet steadied him as he swayed.

'Thank you, brother,' he said. His vision greyed at the edges, and he knew not which of his brothers aided him. 'I have not wielded such power since Bezant.'

'How did you do all that?' asked Forrix.

The interior of the Sharei Maveth was not at all what Atharva had expected. Though there had been hints of considerations beyond the practical in the outward design of the fortress, they had been mere tasters for its interior.

The spaces within were artfully formed and as exquisitely detailed as the dragon palaces of Terra. Its walls were polished smooth as marble and lit with recessed lumen strips. Yet the interior's clean simplicity sacrificed nothing of its defensive nature. Every screwstair turned to the left as it descended, and every onward passageway was laced with blind murder-holes and hidden sally ports.

Perturabo led them to a vaulted chamber deep in the heart of the mountain, a grand hall of gleaming marble veined with gold. Hard-wired servitors laboured at banks of cogitators, and spectral veils of noospheric data shimmered before cliques of Mechanicum adepts conversing in the staccato cadences of Lingua Technis.

Three of its walls were hung with decorative tapestries large enough to fly from the armoured carapace of a Titanicus war-engine. The fourth was inset with a wide oculus screen that put Atharva in mind of the picts he had seen showing the bridge of the *Imperator Somnium*.

Towards the rear of the chamber, wide steps led to a raised mezzanine area where Perturabo had set his command table. Magnus followed his brother up to a space that had the feel of a workshop, the air redolent of hot metal, grease and craft. Sheet-covered workbenches lined walls hung with a host of artificer's tools, and the purpose of a great many were not immediately apparent.

Two Iron Warriors stood at the command table in the centre of the space, haptically shifting data manifests between glowing tags of starship designations. From the crimson stains in their auras, their discussions had been heated.

They looked up as Perturabo arrived and stood to attention.

Perturabo took in the details of the plotter table with a glance and gave a curt nod, indicating Magnus and his warriors should join him. The volume of data presented on the plotter table was bewildering: loading rates, trip times, cargo capacities, fuel reserves, fleet rotations, population influx, food levels, water supply, billeting arrangements and hundreds more variables that played into the evacuation equation.

Even Atharva, who prided himself on his analytical nature and capacity for the unforgiving arithmetic of war, found himself struggling to process the ocean of information displayed.

'My two senior Warsmiths,' said Perturabo, indicating the two Iron Warriors sifting the data. 'Harkor, and Barban Falk.'

To Atharva's eyes, the former had the look of a brawler, thickly waisted and with the majority of his muscle mass layered over his shoulders. A flicker of red danced before Atharva's eyes, a Corvidae sense of bloody destiny.

Falk, however, was finely balanced, and Atharva sensed he was a warrior who might achieve greatness.

'Atharva, my senior Librarius, and Phosis T'kar, one of my First Fellowship captains,' said Magnus.

'Librarius? You still think that is a good idea?' asked Perturabo.

'I do,' said Magnus. 'And Sanguinius agrees with me.'

'Tread lightly, brother,' said Perturabo. 'What happened on Bezant travelled farther than you think. These are uncharted realms. Be sure you know what lies beneath.'

'I will do as you advise and temper my researches with caution,' replied Magnus, and Atharva felt the lightest brush of psychic influence from his primarch, so subtle he was unsure if he'd felt it at all. 'Now, to business, brother. Tell me of the evacuation's progress. Are you on schedule?'

Perturabo blinked and looked up at his brother's use of 'you', but said nothing. If Magnus noticed his brief irritation, he chose not to acknowledge it.

'Barely, and we have little margin for delays,' said Perturabo, turning his attention to the plotter table once more. The primarch called up the manifests and fleet registries for the Legion ships anchored within the upper atmosphere. Data streamed from each entry, a cascade of energy demands, orbital vectors and cargo capacities.

'Your ships are burning fuel at a prodigious rate by coming so close to the pull of Morningstar's gravity,' noted Atharva.

'They are,' agreed Falk. 'It's a necessary trade-off between fuel consumption and overall trip time for the trans-atmospheric vessels. Even a few tens of kilometres less of a round trip makes a considerable difference to the evacuation timetable.'

Perturabo pulled up a host of schematics, spinning wireframe diagrams of the various trans-orbital shuttle variants available to the evacuation effort.

'Leaving aside the *Lux Ferem*, the typical capacity for the trans-orbital conveyors available to us is in the region of three hundred people. Our surface-to-orbit operations can clear around two hundred launches every day, bearing approximately sixty-five thousand people off-world. That gives us a baseline requirement of needing to run thirty days of constant surface-to-orbit flights without interruption to get everyone off-world. And that's without factoring in flight time, air traffic bottlenecks, refuelling or ongoing maintenance. And it takes no consideration of loading and unloading evacuees at either end. Working to best case margins, my initial timetable demands two Terran months to complete operations. We shave *some* time off that as efficiency scales up with repetition, but we'll be doing very well if we get it much below my initial estimate. And that, of course, assumes everyone cooperates and is ready to be moved off Morningstar at regular intervals.'

Magnus smiled. 'I see now why this world needs you.'

'It needs *us*, brother,' said Perturabo. 'Both our Legions are required to make this work.'

'My Lord Perturabo?' said Atharva. 'Might I make an observation?'

'Of course,' said Perturabo. 'You see a flaw?'

Atharva hesitated, well aware of how fluid the foundations were beneath him. Though he had been part of the Great Crusade for a few years only, Perturabo's fearsome reputation for logistical brilliance was already well known.

'Perhaps,' he said.

'Well, spit it out – we're on a tight enough timetable without having to stand on Fifteenth Legion rituals.'

Atharva nodded and dismissed the rotating schematics of the trans-orbital shuttles with a swipe of his hand. He pulled up the fleet registries once more, highlighting each vessel's passenger capacity with haptic gestures.

'The Fourth and Fifteenth Legion fleets comprise enough civilian craft to accommodate between forty and sixty thousand evacuees per vessel. We have thirty-one such ships between us, meaning we have capacity for – on paper – one point six five million people.'

'I can do arithmetic,' said Perturabo. 'What's your point?'

'Even after all that has befallen it, Morningstar's most recent census puts its population at just over two million,' said Atharva. 'Even by stretching supplies, space and available time to breaking point, we cannot evacuate everyone from Morningstar.'

'I am well aware of that, Atharva,' said Perturabo. 'Sadly, not everyone will survive to reach orbit and safety. We've already seen civil disobedience, riots and people who simply don't want to leave.'

'Then a great many people are going to die,' said Atharva.

'A lot of people will end up dead anyway, no matter what we do,' put in Harkor. 'There's no way anyone can organise the mass evacuation of an entire planet without loss of life.'

'Why would anyone not want to leave a doomed world?' asked Phosis T'kar. 'It makes no sense.'

'Hathor Maat and others have reported instances of the populace refusing to relocate in the face of certain death,' said Magnus. 'But I agree, it is vexing why arguments of sound logic and reason should be ignored.'

'The Imperium is better off without such fools,' said Phosis T'kar. 'Why should we waste time and energy trying to help those who will not help themselves?'

Perturabo leaned over the plotting table, and Phosis T'kar recoiled from the flint in his gaze. When the primarch spoke it was with the measured tones of a disappointed teacher.

'For the same reason I would not allow a child to pick flowers on the edge of a cliff, no matter how bright the blooms,' said Perturabo. 'For the same reason I would not let you wander the minefields before this fortress without a Fourth Legion map and the training to interpret it. We must put aside such childish ignorance and do what is right. Now do you understand why we must help as many of Morningstar's people as we can?'

'Yes, Lord Perturabo,' said Phosis T'kar. 'I am in your debt for correcting my erroneous thinking.'

Atharva bit back his amusement. Phosis T'kar was a seasoned scholar, but rarely did he ever admit to being in need of instruction. Even now, in the face of a primarch's rebuke, his aura betrayed a measure of insolence.

Magnus grinned and said, 'Phosis T'kar is at his best when dealing with absolutes. True and false, right and wrong. He excels at unlocking the structures of empirical formulae, but he will never be a moral philosopher or grand debater.'

'Perhaps not, and he's not the first to express such sentiments,' said Perturabo. 'But I'll not have it said we left innocents to die when we could have done something to save them. You and I need to work together, brother. I need every one of your warriors tasked to this world's evacuation, not chasing relics and digging in the dust.'

'One squad diverted to the preservation of knowledge will not affect your timetable,' said Magnus. 'The secrets this world might hold are too precious to be so easily squandered.'

'You really believe there is some ancient knowledge buried in Zharrukin that will explain why Morningstar survived Old Night unscathed?'

'I am certain of it,' said Magnus.

'In anyone else I would say such certainty was arrogant,' sighed Perturabo, letting the data on the plotter table disperse like smoke.

'When have I ever been wrong about such things?' asked Magnus.

'Never,' admitted Perturabo, stepping towards the sheet-covered workbenches at the perimeter of the mezzanine. 'But there is a first time for everything, and I need *all* your warriors on board. But here, I want to show you something.'

The primarch pulled back a white sheet to reveal a haphazard arrangement of half-finished projects, contraptions of mysterious purpose and beautiful arrangements of gears and motors.

'This is my workshop,' said Perturabo.

'It is just as I expected,' said Magnus, delightedly moving from bench to bench to examine the pieces lying around the edges of the workshop. He lifted a sheet of wax paper laid beside a partially completed model of a grand amphitheatre.

'The Thaliakron,' said Magnus. 'You've begun work on it?'

'Not yet,' said Perturabo. 'Soon. When the Crusade is done and we have heroic tales aplenty to fill it with song, then I'll build it. On the mountain across from father's palace.'

'I will be there to see it unveiled,' promised Magnus, and his enthusiasm for his brother's works was genuine and contagious.

He and Perturabo spoke as brothers who had shared every memory from birth to this moment, yet they had known each other for only a few short years. Magnus had once spoken of how he and Perturabo had spent time together on Terra, recovering the relics of a long-dead polymath and unearthing arcana from the forgotten places of Old Earth. Atharva had thrilled to hear such tales, relishing every opportunity to learn more of his gene-sire.

The obvious love between these godlike warriors filled the workspace with a swelling feeling of confraternity, a bond of brotherhood that could never be broken.

'This will be of interest to you, brother,' said Perturabo, holding out a complex arrangement of curved metal, winding mechanisms and adjustable lenses. 'I made a replica of the Antikythera, just like you asked.'

To see so delicate a mechanism in Perturabo's hands seemed incongruous, as most apparatus bearing the stamp of the Iron Warriors that Atharva had seen – save for those within this chamber – had been brutally functional.

'Does it work?'

'I am not entirely sure,' answered Perturabo. 'You never fully explained its intended purpose or how exactly it was designed to function.'

'You've built it,' said Magnus. 'What do *you* think it does?'

'I believe it to be some form of navigational instrument,' said Perturabo, lifting the device to look through one of its eye-pieces. 'It has the look of a sextant once used by seafarers, but with infinitely more dimensions to its operation. What manner of ocean would you be navigating to require such a device?'

'The Great Ocean,' said Magnus. 'It allows even those without our gifts to perceive the realm beyond.'

Perturabo nodded and set down the Antikythera.

'I suspected as much,' he said with a sigh, turning to lift something heavy from another part of his workbench. 'You remember what our father told us in the Hall of Leng? When he spoke of the warp and the danger of looking too deeply into its heart?'

'I do,' said Magnus, 'but this has nothing to do with that.'

'It has *everything* to do with that, as well you know, but we will speak of this later.'

Perturabo's arm swung around and he smashed the delicate mechanisms of the Antikythera with a heavy hammer. The metal of the device buckled and split, the precision-ground lenses shattering into a thousand fragments.

'Brother, no!' cried Magnus as the pieces fell to the floor. 'Why?'

Perturabo replaced the hammer on his workbench and said, 'Because I will play no part in aiding you in delving into things you have been told to leave well alone. Our father knows more than us. He has seen further than us. If He tells us there are regions of the warp into which even He does not dare look, then we are beholden to accept that.'

Magnus stared at the ruined device in disbelief.

Such a piece was the work of a master, a treasure that ought to have been held up as the epitome of the craftsman's art.

Atharva saw Magnus' aura darken, like blood in the water.

'Knowing what you suspected, you could have destroyed the Antikythera at any time after its completion,' said Magnus with cold and controlled anger. 'But you waited until I was here to see you do it. Why?'

'Because you needed to *see* it destroyed to truly understand.'

Magnus let out a breath.

'You have a cruel streak in you, brother,' he said.

'Perhaps,' conceded Perturabo. 'But sometimes cruelty is the only way to make a point so clearly that nobody can ever mistake its intent.'

The sky over Attar's hab-towers burned with clashing magnetics. Hostile stellar radiation was stripping away the planet's atmospheric shield, transforming the night sky into a scintillating borealis of refracted light and billowing storm clouds. Twisted starlight bathed the city with end-of-days radiance.

The highways and mass-conveyance routes out of the city were jammed with every form of transport imaginable as Attar's people fled to Calaena. The organisation of the evacuation was under the aegis of Konrad Vargha's Gubernatorial Guard, but their breathtaking inefficiency had jammed every highway and transit route for tens of kilometres. Mechanicum provosts were attempting to unravel the gridlock, but it was taking time the citizens of Attar did not have.

Lightning stabbed the city with fiery lances over and over again, and its industrial sectors were promethium hellpits of toxic fumes and chemical infernos.

'Beautiful, is it not?' said Magos Tancorix, watching the city die from the laagered safety of his gloss-red Triaros squadron to the north of Attar.

Major Anton Orlov bit back a bitter response and took a calming breath that tasted of fyceline, plastic and burning fuel silos. He wanted to be angry at the Mechanicum adept's singular lack of empathy for the people of Morningstar, but expecting emotion from a machine priest was an exercise in futility. Apparently oblivious to their suffering and loss, he was entirely more concerned with the opportunity to study the anomalous transformation of their planet.

Instead, Orlov said, 'It's hard to think of something that's destroying my world as beautiful.'

'The imminent demise of Morningstar is regrettable, of course,' replied Tancorix without looking up from the array of unfolded work-stations integral to the structure of the Triaros. 'But that does not alter the aesthetics of the storm, Major Orlov, nor the value of the data that will allow us to lessen our current meteorological uncertainty.'

The magos was, physiologically at least, less chimeric than many of his brethren. His face was entirely flesh, yet the back of his skull was a bulbous dome of mnemonic augments, cognitive boosters and coolant pipes.

Every interaction Orlov had with Tancorix reinforced the feeling that any humanity the adept displayed was a veneer, a mask that enabled him to interact with unaugmented mortals. A machine heart beat within his body, as did a ghoulish appreciation for beauty in devastation.

Orlov knew it was pointless to argue with Tancorix, but couldn't help himself.

'Attar was once a prosperous city of seaborne trade from all over Morningstar,' he said, pointing to a windswept headland overlooking the bay. 'I grew up here. When I was young, I used to watch the ships coming in at night from just over there. It was mesmerising to watch the aerial tugs guide the ships in, their prows ablaze with stab-lights and collision markers. I used to imagine they were starships and that I was floating in the void, that I was absolutely alone and free. When I was drafted into the Red Dragons, I missed that view, but any time I had leave, I'd come back here and watch the ships rolling in and out. It gave me a sense of peace and belonging, a sense that as long as the ships kept coming and going all would be well, you understand?'

Orlov looked over at Tancorix, but the magos was intent on the cascades of information scrolling down the Triaros' myriad data-slates.

His sentiment was falling on deaf ears, and he turned his gaze instead to the city's coastline. Far-distant tectonic movement and hydro-volcanoes had split the ocean bedrock and the sea had retreated thousands of kilometres. Beyond the flames engulfing the lower reaches of the city, Attar's vast docks were now towering white cliffs. Attar's once mighty fleet of oceanic harvesters, container vessels and materiel conveyors lay toppled onto their sides, stranded like beached leviathans.

'All that is gone now,' he said. 'Forever.'

'There are others worlds not dissimilar to this one,' said Tancorix, examining a brass-rimmed slate with a jumping needle with a look of puzzlement. He tapped a metallic finger against the glass, but the needle did not steady and yet more joined its frenetic spiking.

'But this one was mine,' said Orlov, 'and I will mourn it.'

Tancorix did not answer, too intent on the vexation his instruments were causing. Orlov saw the adept's eyes widen, which was as close to an exclamation as he ever came.

'What's the matter?' asked Orlov.

'Incoming magnitude readings,' said Tancorix. 'Beyond the capacity of my instrumentation to measure.'

'What does that mean?'

'It suggests an imminent seismic event of catastrophic power.'

'Seismic event – you mean an earthquake?'

'Yes, Major Orlov, an earthquake,' said Tancorix. 'One of unprecedented magnitude and with an epicentre only a few kilometres from where we stand. Omnissiah protect us...'

Sour bile churned in Orlov's belly.

'When?'

'Right now,' said Tancorix as grinding rock and splitting stone twisted the ground and a thrumming bass note split the air.

The headland where Orlov had watched the ships coming and going sheared away, obliterated in a thunderous avalanche. What had once been the seabed ripped wide open, and the burning sectors of Attar tumbled into a hellish fiery chasm.

Morningstar shrugged.

Category 9: CATASTROPHE

[Major scale and duration – multiple populated areas]

FOUR

RUINS • SORCERY • TRAITORS

The last time Magnus had seen such devastation was on Terra. Much of the Throneworld was still in ruins, its many civilisations swept away by continent-cracking weapons, and the monolithic structures of the Imperium yet to be completed. By the time Magnus had come to his father's side, the reconstruction was well under way, but vast swathes of the planet's populace were yet to benefit from the Emperor's worldwide efforts, even so long after Unity had been declared.

It had been a humanitarian crisis of global proportions, but one met with a coordinated response.

No such response would be forthcoming for Attar's people.

The city resembled a scene straight from the imaginings of the ancient dramaturges, the nethermost circle of a terrible realm of torment reserved for the damned.

A new and ferocious night had descended on Attar, the sky sunless as tar-black smoke from the citywide conflagration blotted out the light. Flames from the burning promethium silos that had fallen into the abyssal chasm splitting the waterless bay illuminated the ruins with blood-red firelight. Attar's hab-blocks had tumbled as easily as children's bricks, crashing

71

into one another to form grotesquely intertwined towers of plascrete and steel.

Six Stormbirds touched down on the edge of the city, though it was hard to reconcile the sight before the legionaries as they disembarked as having once *been* a city. All that remained were labyrinthine pathways between groaning ruins, treacherous arrangements of buckled structural elements and precariously balanced heaps of debris.

Magnus disembarked and let out a stifled sob as the scale of the disaster threatened to overwhelm his psychic defences.

Such loss. Such terror.

'So many taken so swiftly,' he said, feeling too much, too deeply. How he wished he could undo what had happened here, to take away the pain and make good all that had been broken.

The Thousand Sons formed up on their primarch and Magnus did his best to shield them from the psychic horror and grief of the city's people.

'How can we possibly navigate *this?*' said Phosis T'kar, staring in wonderment at the smashed city. 'Every schematic we have is useless. Nothing of the city's street plan remains intact.'

'We do not need schematics,' snapped Magnus. 'Use your Corvidae senses and aether-sight to navigate. There are medicae shuttles inbound behind us, so spread out and save as many of these people as you can.'

Another wave of Stormbirds roared overhead, iron-hulled gunships with the distinctive hazard striping of the IV Legion. These were no ordinary craft, but workhorse transports modified to carry construction material. Behind them came a host of fat-bellied Mechanicum conveyers laden with heavy-lifting rigs, tunnellers and rubble excavators.

It had been a battle to convince Perturabo to divert any vessels to the rescue efforts in Attar. The resources were better spent in aiding those already in Calaena, his brother had said. The inference was clear. The deaths here would help balance the unforgiving arithmetic of the Iron Warriors' evacuation timetable.

Perturabo had accounted for great loss of life in the process of the evacuation, and his predictions were being proved uncannily accurate. Magnus almost hated him in that moment, for the first time in his life imagining what it might be like to strike one of his brothers.

The moment had passed and Magnus reluctantly conceded the necessity for such hard calculations, though it still sat ill with him to simply write off the inhabitants of Attar as statistics on a balance sheet of life and death.

But he had seen an opportunity amid the streams of information coming from Magos Tancorix's data-gathering station just beyond Attar. A name that had seen Perturabo finally authorise a rescue mission.

'Move out,' said Magnus. 'I give you leave to use your powers wherever you can to help the Iron Warriors.'

'Is that wise, my lord?' asked Phosis T'kar. 'There are already... *mutterings* of what we can do.'

'Do not argue with me,' said Magnus. 'I will not let people die when we might save them. Now go!'

Phosis T'kar nodded as Magnus turned and walked away.

'Where are you going, my lord?' asked Phosis T'kar.

'I am going to find Konrad Vargha,' said Magnus.

'The planetary governor's bio-tagging is non-functional,' said Phosis T'kar. 'It is likely he is dead.'

'He is alive,' said Magnus. 'I know it.'

'Even if that is true, how will you find him among this?'

'How little you know of me,' said Magnus. 'Trust me, my son – there is nowhere he can be that I cannot find him.'

* * *

Swirling dust hung in the air in choking veils, coating everything in white and burying the dead in ashen shrouds. Magnus let himself perceive the world in hues of psychic resonance, overlaying his already superlative vision with echoes unseen by most mortals.

Emergency sirens wailed in the distance, as if lamenting the destruction around them. Stone split stone with grinding slowness, and steel reinforcement shrieked as it bent and snapped. Bloody survivors wandered numbly through the wreckage of their homes, vainly calling the names of loved ones and family members.

The city was moaning with all its voices.

Muffled cries of wounded men and women echoed in the fallen canyons of broken buildings, but these were all too few. Attar's destruction had come so swiftly that most of its populace had died without even knowing what was happening.

Magnus pushed swiftly through the ruins, every one of his physical and subtle senses extended to guide him.

Konrad Vargha was, unusually for Imperial governors, a native of the compliant world. Morningstar's people remembered Old Earth and Vargha had willingly embraced the newly arrived Imperial forces. His fervour had so impressed the expeditionary fleet commanders and Terran envoys that it had seemed only logical to allow him to remain in command of Morningstar.

His death could not be simply chalked up as a statistic.

Magnus had only met Governor Vargha once, but that was enough. The mental imprint of a mind was as distinctive as a genetic trace or a fingerprint. More so, as no two minds – even those of genetic clones – were identical.

Even that fleeting contact would be enough to find the man.

Magnus paused in the shadow of a ruined structure that might once have been a commerce building. It leaned at a dangerous angle, its facade sagging like wet parchment. Spalling shards of stone fell from its roof and broken glass littered the ground before it.

'You are still alive,' said Magnus. 'I know it.'

He had not lied to Phosis T'kar, not really. Magnus had no direct knowledge of whether or not Konrad Vargha was alive or not, but upon their first meeting he had experienced a brief vision of the man, weeping and soiled aboard a Legion gunship as it soared beneath burning storms.

That was no guarantee of anything, of course. No vision could be entirely trusted, for the pathways into the future branched and divided so rapidly and unexpectedly that nothing was ever set in stone. But it was enough to convince Magnus that a rescue effort into Attar was worth attempting.

With a twist of thought, he detached his subtle body from his flesh, letting it drift free in a nimbus of dazzling, silver-threaded light.

Instantly, the screaming thought-forms of thousands of people stabbed into his mind like hot knives. He could not shut them out, and nor would he even if that were possible. The least he could do was share a measure of the city's pain.

The ruins sang with the psychic howls of the dead and the dying, a wasteland of souls untimely ripped from their bodies. Anguish filled its broken streets, a paean to suffering that clawed at the walls between worlds and a siren song to the *things* that lived beyond.

He rose high above the city, seeing further and deeper without a cage of blood and bone to confine him. The monumental scale of Attar's suffering was laid out before him, a shattered wasteland of stone and glass that had once been a thriving city.

'How fragile is our grip on all we have achieved,' said Magnus, 'when everything can be swept away in the moment between two breaths.'

The aetheric realm was densely populated; thousands of

red-limned ghosts drifted through the city on unseen winds, dead souls now lost in a place they had once known well. Magnus hardened himself against their fear and confusion. They were beyond any help he could offer, their energies already being drawn into the empyrean.

Amid such a vista of death and cacophony of suffering, the living were bright spots of light, candles flickering all too briefly in the darkness. Magnus pushed aside his grief and sought one particular light amid the anguish.

He summoned the mental patterns he had felt when Vargha first introduced himself. Magnus could read the thoughts of mortals in the blink of an eye, but usually refrained from doing so out of respect for their privacy and the knowledge that their skulls were too cluttered with insignificant flotsam and jetsam to be of much interest.

Konrad Vargha's implanted bio-tracker might be non-functional, but his mind trace was a steady light burning in the heart of Attar. Magnus swooped over the city, past burning hab-structures folded like pasteboard and over flaming ravines that had once been grand parks.

He felt his legionaries moving through the city, flaring geysers of psychic power as they melted steel, lifted impossible weights and eased pain with their gifts. Beyond the city, the hard grey souls of the Iron Warriors were untangling the unholy mess Vargha's troops had made of the evacuation: widening roadways, clearing wrecks and restoring the flow of traffic to Calaena.

Only a fraction of Attar's people would be saved, but how could any of them forgive themselves had they turned a blind eye to the suffering because it was statistically irrelevant?

Magnus pushed that thought aside, following the light of Konrad Vargha's life until he finally found the man. His body was trapped within an overturned Rhino transport vehicle, its hull partially crushed beneath the wall of a collapsed foundry.

The crew of the Rhino were dead, but Vargha was still alive, his aura jagged with pain and frustration.

Magnus fixed the location in his mind and sped back to where his physical form awaited, inviolate within a kine shield in the shadow of the commerce building. He sighed as he returned to the weight of his physical form.

How wondrous would it be to exist forever as a being of light and wonder, without need for corporeal form? What evolutionary processes or transformative act would be needed to achieve such a sublime state of being?

A question for another time.

Perhaps he would call a symposium on the subject once they were done with Morningstar.

Little remained to indicate Morningstar's first city had once stood here. The sky was unusually clear and the air still: a moment of rare silence on a world tearing itself apart from within. From all around Morningstar, ever-worsening reports were being received of calamitous climate changes, continental-scale earthquakes and magna-storms of such intensity that they scoured the land back to the bedrock.

Atharva's visor read-out told him he was standing exactly where he had seen Magnus walk from the storm, but little indication remained of that.

Zharrukin had all but vanished, the earth scorched more thoroughly than any invading army could hope to salt it. The walls of its great structures were gone, scattered like a fallen empire with naught but dust as its legacy.

All that remained was an undulating wasteland of smashed plascrete that looked to have fallen from a great height, twisted rebars jutting from exposed foundations like desert bracken.

'It's all gone,' said Niko Ashkali, bending to scoop a handful of the city's powdered remains. 'It is all dust.'

'What?'

'I said there is nothing left,' said Ashkali, standing and brushing her hands together. She glanced over her shoulder to where a single stripped-down Stormbird, so skeletal and reduced it really deserved another designation, settled in the ash behind them. 'I am not sure why we are here. Are your warriors not required to aid the evacuation efforts?'

'I've been wondering the same thing,' said Hathor Maat, appearing at Atharva's side and scanning their desolate, empty surroundings. 'Why *are* we here?'

Atharva masked his irritation at Hathor Maat's loose tongue. He had not served with the warrior before now, but could read enough of his Pavoni aura to know he was vain even beyond most of that strutting Fellowship.

Along with Atharva and Hathor Maat, four other legionaries had been assigned to this mission. They were all from different companies and squads, to better disguise that they were no longer with their units. This mission reeked of subterfuge and Atharva detested subterfuge.

But the order came directly from his primarch.

Magnus had halted Atharva moments before departing for Attar and given him alternative orders.

'Return to Zharrukin,' said the primarch.

'Zharrukin?' he had asked. 'The city is gone. There is nothing left of it.'

Magnus shook his head, and the intensity of his gaze was unsettling. 'You are wrong, Atharva. There is more yet to discover, I know it.'

'The storm will have taken whatever remained of the city.'

'No, something lies beneath,' said Magnus. 'I did not have time to find it before, but you will if you go now.'

'What am I to look for?'

Magnus paused, as though turning his mind inwards.

'Look for the sign of a feathered arrowhead,' he said at last. 'It will guide you.'

'What does that mean?'

Magnus grinned, and Atharva felt himself mirroring the gesture. 'I do not know, but you will get to discover something wondrous, my son. Truth be told, I am jealous.'

Despite such a prospect, Atharva could not shake the notion they were doing something deceitful by being here, something that might have grave consequences. Was that Corvidae instinct or guilt at being here instead of helping with the planetary relief efforts?

He did not know, and that troubled him.

Atharva shook off his nagging feelings of unease and walked through the eerily quiet ruins, using the cracked foundations and sheared nubs of structural columns to form a mental map of the vanished city.

'Spread out,' he said. 'Look for anything that could conceivably be a feathered arrowhead.'

'What's that?' asked Hathor Maat.

'Something that will guide us,' said Atharva. 'Now do it. And report in as soon as you see anything that matches that description.'

Hathor Maat and the others set off in various directions, quartering the ruins and hunting for something whose meaning was beyond them. Atharva watched them go and turned to Ashkali.

'Conservator Ashkali.'

'Niko.'

'Of course, I forgot,' said Atharva. 'Tell me, does a feathered arrowhead design have any particular cultural or symbolic resonance on Morningstar?'

'Perhaps,' said Ashkali, bending to draw a circle in the dust with her fingertip. Then, with five quick strokes, she drew a star within it.

'Tell me what you see,' she said.

'The planetary sigil of Morningstar.'

Ashkali swept away the left and right points of the star.

'Just over thirty years ago, some agri-settlers in the Laveyan Grottos uncovered some artefacts that appeared to date from a time before Old Night.'

'What kinds of artefacts?'

'Just scraps, really,' said Ashkali, tapping a finger against her lip as she sorted through her memories. 'Partially decayed cloth that might have been uniforms, metal fragments and smashed pieces of machinery. But the best-preserved piece was what looked like the remains of a helmet.'

'A warrior's helmet?'

'I do not believe so. It appeared to be a primitive environment helmet from a void suit. Here, I'll show you.'

Atharva leaned down as Ashkali produced a data-slate from her hip-pouch and began scrolling through grainy imagery pulled from an archived database.

'Where are you…?' she said, flipping through scans of crumbling relics pulled from the earth of Morningstar. 'Ah, there it is.'

The image quality was poor, the lousy atmospherics disrupting the connection, but Atharva felt a thrill of familiarity as he stared at the wavering image.

The helm had once been bright yellow, but had faded with age and damage. A painted insignia above the cracked visor was still visible – faint, but unmistakably that of a vectored arrow encircled by a stylised ring and wreath that could easily be interpreted as feathers.

'Some of the oldest settlers claim *this* was Morningstar's original sigil, that the others points of the star were added later,' said Ashkali.

'They may very well be correct.'

'You know this symbol?'

'A variant form of it, yes.'

'Where did you see it? On Terra?'

'Yes. When the eastern ethnarchs fell, the Thousand Sons marched across the cindered remains of the Dragon Nations, preserving and learning all we could of that land's ancient history and culture. Much had already been lost in the fires of self-immolation, but in the ruins of Ba-Shu, we found the remains of a storage facility for rockets intended to bear atomic warheads. However, that did not appear to be its original designation – its true purpose was a launch station for trans-orbital craft, perhaps the first to breach the solar system. Some of the walls had a faded versions of this symbol painted on them.'

'I see,' said Ashkali. 'But why would you send your men to look for such a symbol now?'

'Because I have been told it will guide us.'

'Guide us to what?'

'I do not know,' said Atharva. 'My primarch believes this city yet keeps secrets from us. This symbol will guide us to them.'

No sooner had the words left his lips than he felt a flare of emotion from Hathor Maat. The legionary's excitement was palpable, his Pavoni affiliations transmitting a measure of it to Atharva. He pushed himself into the fourth Enumeration to counter it with reason.

+Atharva, you have to see this...+

+What is it? What have you found?+

+Best you come and see for yourself.+

Ashkali saw the change in his body language and cocked her head to one side.

'What is it?'

'We've found something,' said Atharva.

They set off through the dead city towards where Hathor Maat was waiting within the remains of a vast structure, easily capable of housing an entire vehicle regiment. Its roof was gone, and only the lower reaches of its reinforced walls remained intact.

Hathor Maat stood at the edge of what looked like an elevator shaft for bringing vehicles up from a subterranean hangar. He turned as they approached, and his aura was alight with dancing colours: greens, golds and blues.

'What is it?' asked Atharva, as he and Ashkali picked a path through the rubble towards him.

Hathor Maat simply pointed downwards.

Atharva reached the edge of the shaft and leaned over.

Bare plascrete walls plunged hundreds of metres into the earth, and portions of a buckled metal stairwell were bolted around its perimeter. Cracked lumen globes stuttered, telling Atharva that power still flowed somewhere below.

At the base of the shaft was a curved expanse of bare metal, formed of riveted iron sheets. Its surface was rusted after centuries or more spent beneath the ground, and at its centre was a gleaming hatch with an armourglass portal.

'What is this?' began Ashkali.

'Those are hull plates,' said Hathor Maat. 'Of a starship!'

'It is so much more than that,' said Atharva, seeing the icon from the damaged helmet emblazoned on the sealed hatch.

'What do you mean?' asked Ashkali.

'I mean, this is a Terran colony ship.'

Magnus ran through the ruins of Attar like a hunting beast on the scent of its prey. He followed Konrad Vargha's psychic trace, a magnesium-bright lodestone burning its location into his mind.

Traversing the city was a vision of torment.

Wherever he looked he saw suffering: corpses scattered throughout the ruins with arms spread wide as though to welcome this armageddon; blinded survivors wandering the ruins in shock; men and women on their hands and knees, vainly trying to dig through the rubble of their homes. Truly, this was a vision of the underverse Russ had once spoken of in an unguarded moment, when they had taken shelter from sciomantic lightning on the Bugulma-Belebey Upplands.

He moved at speed, letting nothing slow him: not towering piles of rubble that would have taken cohorts of bulk-servitors hours to remove, nor fires fuelled by endless reservoirs of promethium. The Great Ocean filled him with the power to smash aside debris, transmute steel to mist and render towering infernos into freezing rain.

Like a god, he moved through the rubble of Attar, wreathed in light as he blazed a path through the devastation.

And like any divine figure, he attracted followers.

Some simply saw him as a way out, others as a worker of miracles. Yet more saw him as a saviour, an armoured warrior god come to lead them from this nightmare to safety.

Singly and in tiny groups they came, stumbling and weeping in his wake as he forged a path through the ruins. That his course took him deeper into Attar seemed to matter not at all – that he moved with purpose and mystical light was all that counted. Magnus did not dissuade them; by following him they stood a better chance of surviving.

By the time he finally reached the source of Konrad Vargha's mind trace, over a hundred desperate, bloodied souls and grief-maddened wretches had latched on to him. They followed in a ragged host, beseeching him with appeals to help find their loved ones, to dig their children from the rubble, to restore life to dead wives and husbands, to somehow reverse the catastrophe that had swallowed their city. As every one of their cries came to him, he vowed he would plumb the depths of the Great Ocean so that he would never have to hear such cries in vain again.

Ahead was the smouldering wreck of the crushed Rhino, its red-painted hull buckled but still intact. It sat in the centre of a cratered roadway, half fallen into a spreading pool of shimmering oil and rainbow-sheened promethium leaking from the ruptured silos of the refinery.

Magnus ran forwards, drawing the power of the Great Ocean into him and freezing the dangerously flammable liquid to ice. Webbed frost spread across the Rhino's hull, and Magnus altered the chemical composition of the air around the vehicle to eliminate the oxygen and keep any sparks from igniting the explosive vapours.

A gentle kine barrier kept the wailing survivors from his back as he pulled open the Rhino's hull with his bare hands and threw the torn metal aside. The vehicle's interior was awash with blood. The Rhino's crew had been killed on impact, the hard edges of the interior structure smashing them apart as the vehicle rolled.

Only Vargha had survived thanks to his placement in the rear of the vehicle, the portion shielded from the worst of the crash by the engine block. The planetary governor was a broad-shouldered and powerful man, his patrician features the result of careful breeding. He lay sprawled across a vox-caster console that was somehow still functional, his shattered legs trapped by the crushed drive mechanism.

Magnus wove an intricate pattern in the air, and the metal pinning the governor in place disassembled into its constituent parts. Hundreds of cogs, gears, spindles and panels floated into the air and fell away as Magnus unmade the machinery with a fractional expenditure of power.

Vargha slumped as the weight pinning his legs was removed. Blood pumped from his torn flesh and he tried to scream, but there was no air to draw into his lungs. His eyes bulged in agony and from lack of oxygen. He glared at Magnus as he was lifted from the Rhino, as if the primarch were the source of his pain.

The crowd gathered around Magnus dropped to their knees at the sight of the governor's rescue. Magnus walked through them, bearing Vargha in his arms as they raised their arms towards him. The governor's thigh bones had been shattered like glass, and the base of his spine was a pulped mass of marrow and bone. Blood soaked Magnus' chest as he eased his power into Vargha's ruined flesh.

Aetheric energy raced throughout the governor's body, renewing torn blood vessels, restoring destroyed nerves and mending bones that were little better than powdered fragments. Vargha screamed as his nerves awoke to fire, both his femurs cracking as the bones regrew and were made whole.

The pain was too much, and his eyes rolled back in his head as unconsciousness claimed him. Magnus nodded, feeling the man's aura settle as swiftly growing flesh knitted over the wounds where, only moments before, splintered nubs of bone had jutted.

He turned as he heard the rumble of engines, heavy-duty military grade. A wall of debris blocking the roadway collapsed as a colossal super-heavy tank equipped with a siege-grade dozer blade bludgeoned its way through.

A Baneblade, a mobile battle fortress armed to the teeth with the deadliest weapons mankind had yet devised.

An avalanche of rubble cascaded into the street as its enormous mass cleared a path for the smaller vehicles behind it – a mix of Rhinos, Chimeras and Executioners. All were painted in the colours of the Red Dragons, and Magnus nodded to himself. At least the survivors gathered around him had a means of escape now.

The Baneblade slewed to a halt, and the cupola on its topside opened. A soldier in the tough canvas and leather of a tanker's tunic emerged, his face obscured by a visored helmet and rebreather apparatus. A golden pin depicting the encircled star that was this planet's sigil glittered at his lapel. Something in its orientation seemed strangely relevant to Magnus, though he could not say exactly why.

'Get those vehicles over here,' he ordered. 'There are survivors that need transport to safety.'

'Is that Governor Vargha?' asked the soldier, his voice muffled by the rebreather.

'It is, but I will carry him out. Open your assault ramps and help these people.'

The soldier touched his hand to the side of his helmet and nodded at whatever order he was being given. He dropped back inside the Baneblade and slammed the hatch shut behind him.

Seconds later, the vehicles opened fire.

FIVE

RAPTURE • HAIL SHAITAN • WHAT DID YOU DO?

Overlapping repulsor fields from the fleet of tugs holding station overhead were interfering with the operation of Ahriman's war-plate. He vented air from his gorget, easing the pressure within his helmet.

Forty of the heavy-duty tugs, each little more than a servitor-cockpit bolted to a vastly powerful gravitic engine, strained like hounds on the leash, poised to haul the *Lux Ferem*'s magnificent bulk into the air once its cargo bays were fully loaded. Once the mass-conveyor's own engines could bear its colossal weight, they would detach and return to the space port.

Enormous ramps led from the ground to the *Lux Ferem*'s cavernous embarkation decks, and thousands of people marched into its belly with their heads down. They bore all their worldly possessions on their backs, and every one of them turned for a last, fleeting look at their doomed home world.

'This is the last batch for loading,' said Forrix, consulting a data-slate filled with names and numbers.

'The balance sheet of survival,' said Ahriman. 'Those who will live to tell fond remembrances of their lost planet in the decades to come.'

'They are the lucky ones,' said Forrix. 'They have fallen on the correct side of the equation and will get to live.'

Casting his senses out over the refugees being guided up the ramps like livestock, Ahriman doubted any of them felt lucky, but refrained from pointing that out.

'It all comes down to numbers with the Fourth, doesn't it?'

'Of course,' said Forrix. 'Any fool knows that is how wars are won, through superior logistics, planning and the proper assessment of risk.'

'What of courage? What of honour and sacrifice? Do they not also play a part in winning wars?'

'Some,' allowed Forrix. 'But far less than you would imagine. The greatest warrior of a Legion cannot shoot if his bolter is without ammunition. The deadliest super-heavy tank cannot crush the enemy beneath its tracks without oceans of fuel, and the heaviest artillery cannot pound fortifications without a constant supply of shells. The duty of an Iron Warrior is to win any war as quickly and efficiently as possible.'

'I know you are correct, but to reduce war to numbers and equations feels like a mistake,' said Ahriman. 'When individual lives are no more than numbers, it becomes easier to forget that they are living beings. Yes, plan a war in this way, but do not fight it like that.'

'You are sentimental, Ahzek,' said Forrix, his words coming out like a warning. 'So I hope you never have to face an enemy that thinks like *my* Legion. It would not go well for you.'

Ahriman recoiled at the idea of taking arms against brother legionaries. That Forrix could even consider such a thing spoke volumes as to his Legion's outlook. What manner of debates must go on in the sanctums of the Iron Warriors?

He put aside abhorrent thoughts of war between brothers, trying not to let the disturbing logic of Forrix's words take hold in his heart. The refugees filed past and he saw the same carved-in numbness on every face.

'A pall of defeat hangs over them,' he said.

'Understandable,' answered Forrix. 'There are more reports of random attacks in the streets. Violence is on the increase beyond the city limits and on the transit routes.'

'Is there no more we can do to keep these people safe?'

'There is, but at what cost?'

'Surely no cost is too high?'

'You forget we are against a ticking clock, Ahzek,' pointed out Forrix. 'Too much security at the city perimeter means fewer people escape Morningstar, whereas no security gets more people to the ships quicker, but increases the risk of hostile infiltration. Lord Perturabo has calculated the optimal balance between speed of entry and the risk of allowing hostiles through the outer cordons. This is it.'

Ahriman knew Forrix was correct, yet he could not help but rail against the notion of an individual's survival being a matter of unfeeling calculations. The members of the nascent Order of Ruin within the Thousand Sons were also fascinated with numbers, but their interest leaned more towards cosmological significance.

This was different.

This was the end result of a cold, logical, brute-force arithmetic of death.

'But you could speed this process, couldn't you?' said Forrix, and Ahriman needed no psychic powers to know what the Iron Warrior was going to say next. 'Your Legion's... abilities. You could employ them to look into these peoples' minds and identify those with hostile intent.'

Ahriman shook his head. 'You have no idea of the complexity of what you are suggesting.'

'I've seen you do it already, right before that madman's host attacked the crowds on the Boulevard of Firmaments.'

'That was different.'

'How so?'

'He was one mind among many, his emotions monstrously heightened, and his thoughts like a beacon on a clear night.'

'Are you saying you cannot do it?'

'No, only that such a feat is not as easy as you imagine.'

'But you *can* do it?'

'Yes.'

'Show me,' said Forrix, nodding towards the refugees.

Ahriman saw he wasn't going to escape without a demonstration of his powers, as if they were some kind of parlour trick instead of the result of years of study and training.

'Very well,' he said, easing his mind into the Enumerations.

He had not been entirely honest with Forrix. What he was attempting was simple enough, but the Thousand Sons were yet to reveal the full extent of what they could do. Fear of the unknown was an all too human characteristic, even among the Legions, and Magnus had yet to decide how and when such a revelation would be made.

Ahriman slowed his breathing and allowed the confused, tangled morass of mortal thoughts to wash over him. A yammering tide of internal monologues broke like a surge tide against his mental defences. It was easy enough to withstand – mortal thoughts were like the yapping of an irritating animal, full of basic wants and needs, and devoid of the clarity that only Prospero's teachings could instil.

Forrix's mind stood out like an inviolable rock in a tempestuous ocean, untouched and impermeable. Ahriman resisted the temptation to brush the Iron Warrior's mind, already knowing what he would see: hard-edged purpose and certainty, unbending devotion to duty and a slavish obedience to his primarch.

Blessed is the mind too small for doubt, thought Ahriman.

The sentiment was unworthy of him. Forrix was a warrior

of great honour and courage, a legionary whom he would be proud to have at his side when the fires of the last great battle were closing in.

And, more than that, Ahriman suspected he and Forrix were becoming friends, which had surprised him, until he thought of Magnus and Perturabo's friendship.

Were they subconsciously emulating their gene-sires? Did a primarch's behaviour have so profound an impact on his sons that they unwittingly aped it? Taking that thought to its furthest logical extreme offered some intriguing prospects for moral debate.

If a primarch was to exhibit morally questionable behaviour, would some of his sons blindly follow him? Would all of them?

Would Ahriman?

As if that thought were a key to some infernal lock of the future, Ahriman's neck snapped back and he looked to the sky in horror as his Corvidae senses flared. An agonising veil of red fell over his sight, a bloody eclipse of things yet to be.

Flames burned from here to the horizon.

A world ablaze.

Figures writhed in the firelight. Legionaries in the livery of the Iron Warriors, impossibly alive and in endless torment. He saw Forrix, his skin blackened and flesh running like wax as a torrent of impacts tore him apart.

Screaming in an agony that would never end.

The vast, cyclopean bulk of something impossible to comprehend loomed over its burning empire, the sound of its laughter screeching, cruel and inhuman. Metal glinted in the sky from a thousand falling blades. Liquid fire rained down in a deluge and mountains ran molten beneath it.

The world tilted as if at some immense impact.

A hammer of the gods slamming down.

The impact threw Ahriman from his vision and he cried out

as a hideous sensation of vertigo blurred his vision. He felt himself falling until Forrix caught him and lowered him to his knees. The Iron Warrior's aura blazed with readiness to fight.

'What did you see?' demanded Forrix. 'Is there an imminent threat?'

Ahriman tried to answer, but the horror of the destruction he had witnessed rendered him mute. It made him want to weep, to tear his hair and curse the stupidity of man.

'I saw you die. I saw this place destroyed,' he said, steadying himself with a palm flat on the ground.

'Destroyed? How?'

'I do not know,' said Ahriman, fighting to slow his racing heartbeat. 'But it was no vision of natural catastrophe – it was an *engineered* doom.'

'Engineered? You mean an attack?'

Ahriman nodded, blinking as he looked up and the world-consuming fires of his aether vision faded. The natural streetscape and the slow-moving columns of refugees swam back into focus.

'What I saw… It was an apocalypse of man's own devising.'

'When will this apocalypse happen?'

'Soon.'

'Soon? When exactly?' demanded Forrix, his Legion's hatred of ambiguity shining through in his bellicose aura.

'I cannot say *exactly!*' snapped Ahriman.

He heard the click of Forrix opening the vox to his fellow legionaries and reached up to grip the Iron Warrior's arm.

'Wait… The men who brought the fire…' he said. 'I sensed their minds. They were not filled with hate, not at all…'

'Then what? Madness?'

Ahriman felt the frightened stares of curious onlookers and sensed their unease at the sight of a fallen legionary.

Which of them would it be?

'Of a sort,' he said, rising unsteadily to his feet, mentally reciting the Mandalic Catechism to centre himself.

'What do you mean?' asked Forrix.

'It was love,' said Ahriman. 'It was *rapture*.'

The lascannon blast struck Magnus just below his heart.

His surprise was total. He had no time to raise a kine shield. Pain ripped through him.

The beam burned with the heat of a sun. A stinking mist of instantly vaporised blood and tissue enveloped him. He inhaled a draught of red mist, an aerosolised breath of his own body.

Magnus had never been hurt before. Not truly.

He had allowed himself to suffer cuts and bruises when it suited his purposes to allow his sons to see him bleed alongside them, but nothing like this. He had even suffered more severe wounds to better understand the experience, but that had been entirely controlled.

Only as the superheated beam destroyed his flesh did he fully appreciate how cowardly that had been.

He dropped Konrad Vargha as the supplicants surrounding him scattered in screaming panic. High-calibre shells from sponson-mounted assault weapons raked them, cutting down a score of people almost immediately and wounding dozens more.

The Red Dragons were slaughtering their own people.

Anger gave Magnus focus and he drew a kine shield about him as easily as a mortal man might pull a cloak tighter in a cold wind. The second lascannon shot bent around him like light through water. He ripped the weapon from its sponson mount with a flick of thought. Fire erupted from the Baneblade's flank as arcing lightning flared from ruptured power lines.

Magnus felt the elation of the mind at the gunner's position behind the super-heavy tank's prow-mounted cannon. His arm pistoned out as its shortened barrel blazed with fire and smoke. The siege shell was moving at fifteen hundred metres per second, but Magnus swept his arm to the side and the shell slammed into the foundry wall behind him.

It detonated in a devastating blast, and the already weakened walls of the ruined structure came down in a roaring cascade of debris. Magnus heard screams as people taking shelter from the rogue vehicles were crushed by falling masonry. He threw kine shields over as many as he could, but it wasn't enough to save them all.

The ground heaved as an aftershock rumbled far below the surface, toppling what few structures were left standing. Magnus took that power and drew it into himself, grunting as the world's pain suffused his flesh. He thrust his hand forwards and an up-armoured Rhino crumpled as though in the grip of an invisible Titan. Metal shrieked and spat fire as the vehicle's entire mass was compacted down to a perfect sphere no more than a metre in diameter.

Magnus clenched his fist and swung his arm to the side, slamming the unimaginably dense mass of metal like a wrecking ball. He smashed another Rhino flat before hammering the wreckage into a pair of Chimeras. The vehicles hurtled through the air, vanishing over the cliffs of the sea docks.

More las-bolts and solid slugs raked him. Most skidded away from his psi-shield, but others clipped his armour, grazed his flesh or – in one case – exploded against his ribs.

Magnus fell to one knee, his protection dissolving into scraps of hard air. Another shot took him high on the shoulder, spinning him around and almost knocking him onto his back. Iridescent blood sheeted his armour, the metal reshaping itself around the wound.

The Executioner swerved around the wrecks of its fellows,

looking to flank him. Its turret cannon swung around as its hull weapons fired into the sheltering civilians.

The Baneblade came straight at him.

It ground over the smashed remains of a headless statue, crushing the likeness of an Imperial grandee to powder beneath its titanic weight. The turret-mounted battle cannon lowered and Magnus sensed the crew within – the driver alight with manic glee, the commander exhilarated at the prospect of slaying so mighty a foe, its gunners vying for the chance to take the kill-shot. Their auras blazed with the passions common to all mortals in the crucible of combat.

Magnus rammed his power into their skulls, tearing at the myriad webs of synaptic connections within. They screamed in his mind as he twisted their thoughts like a team of riggers hauling on a mainsail, making them his puppets.

The Baneblade swung about and slammed into the flanking Executioner, crumpling its red-painted hull and driving it up onto one track. The tank tipped over and the Baneblade punched it forwards twenty metres until finally driving it hard against a wall of debris. The super-heavy tank's tracks ripped up rock and dust as the driver gunned the engines. Reeking smoke belched from its protesting drive unit.

Magnus sent a pulse of thought to the Baneblade's gunners and both tanks vanished in a series of percussive fireballs as they fired every weapon system. The Executioner was obliterated instantly, and the force of the point-blank blasts ripped open the Baneblade's glacis. It rolled back from the carnage, its front armour peeled open and thick black smoke belching from within.

Screaming bodies tumbled from the flames.

Magnus let them burn.

He saw the outline of the last tank through the smoke and fire of the Baneblade's death. He expected it to retreat, to flee the destruction, but instead it roared towards him, spraying mass-reactive rounds from its cupola mount. Magnus turned them to wisps of perfumed air and lifted the tank from the ground with an outstretched hand.

The tracks spun and the fusillade of gunfire continued. Magnus stood immobile before a wall of burning tanks, surrounded by the dead and the dying. The insanity of the last moments filled his mind with a fury like nothing he had ever known.

He pulled the tank apart: every rivet unmoored, every screw unthreaded, every welded seam undone. Nothing was destroyed or damaged, and with enough time and patience, a Techmarine could have rebuilt the tank.

At the heart of the disassembled vehicle, the tank's crewmen drifted like a pair of spacefarers adrift in zero gravity. The gunner reached for his sidearm. Magnus increased his core temperature by a thousand degrees between heartbeats. The man exploded in a flash of superheated, blood-rich vapour.

He pulled the driver of the vehicle towards him, bolts and washers spinning away as his flailing arms tried to resist the inexorable force reeling him in. He held the man before him in the air and ripped his helmet off with a thought. The face before him was ordinary, but what had he expected to see? The face of a monster? Someone who could be seen to be evil for what he had done?

No, this was simply a man. His skin had the pallid, oily sheen common to tankers, but Magnus saw none of the awe and dread common to mortals when they first laid eyes on him. Even Roboute and Rogal, primarchs of a comprehensible nature to mortal sensibilities, still elicited wonder.

'Finish me!' he screamed. 'I must die!'

'You will die,' promised Magnus. 'But first you are going to tell me why you were trying to kill the planetary governor.'

The man laughed, his system thick with intoxicants, his mind afire with burning certainty. 'The Great Dying is upon us,' he said, the words pouring out of him in a rush. 'The end of days is to be welcomed, not feared! You and your devil warriors are keeping us from the rapture we were promised when the Night of Nights fell upon the galaxy. The chosen people were lifted up, but our world endured. We were kept from our rightful place at the side of the Stormlord. We have kept to the faith and this is our time, as was foretold in the *Book of Leviathan*. We will die in the fire as Morningstar falls and we will be reborn. So it was written, so shall it be. Hail Shaitan!'

Now Magnus understood the man's lack of awe. This was no confessional; it was the preaching of a zealot. His sense of wonder was already invested in a power beyond the reach of measure or accountability, an invented power that could never be called into question because it could never be seen or touched.

Blind faith was his armour against any doubt.

'I came here to save you people,' said Magnus.

'We do not *need* saving,' spat the man. 'We do not *want* saving. You are a devil, one of the fallen angels, and the Stormlord's retribution will be mighty when His fire turns on you and your faithless sons.'

'I almost feel sorry for you,' said Magnus. 'You have been fed banal lies and told it was golden truth.'

'No, for I have seen the truth. When death takes me, I will be numbered among the blessed.'

'You think death will be your salvation?'

'I know it will be.'

'Then I am doing you a favour,' said Magnus, and snapped the man's neck.

He dropped the corpse and let the suspended parts of the Rhino fall the ground. They clattered to the ruins in a rain of glittering metal as the few survivors of the treacherous attack emerged in ones and twos from the flaming rubble.

Magnus ignored them, too focused on trying to restore his aetheric balance. The power of the world he had taken into his body was still there, its vast and awesome potential like pressure building behind a cracking dam. With such power he could achieve almost anything, and the temptation to wield it was almost too great to resist, for what craven heart could feel and see infinity then turn from it?

He took in a furnace-hot breath, letting the pain, anger, frustration and the savage pleasure he had taken in the act of murder settle within his flesh. This borrowed power would likely destroy him without the proper ritual cleansing to allow it to dissipate back into the warp.

No, the repercussions of this day would not easily fade.

The survivors of Attar flowed around Magnus like water around a rock. They bent to retrieve Konrad Vargha and bore him between them like a fallen martyr. The man groaned in his unconsciousness, kept from agony by Magnus' Pavoni arts.

Magnus exhaled slowly, letting his senses spread over the city once more. He felt the presences of his legionaries, already working their way back to the Stormbirds with as many other survivors as they could rescue.

+My lord?+ Phosis T'kar sensed his master's damaged presence and was instantly aware that something singular and profound had occurred. +Are you... hurt?+

+Not in any way that matters. Ready the gunships. We are leaving this city.+

+Do you have the planetary governor?+

+I do,+ said Magnus.

+Is he alive?+

+He is,+ said Magnus. +Fix on my location. I have other survivors.+

+Yes, my lord. On our way.+

Magnus felt Phosis T'kar's confusion. The warrior had been

told that his primarch was all but a god, immortal and undying, a wise and noble exemplar of all that was good in humanity.

Now he knew different.

So, too, did Magnus.

'Do we open it?' asked Hathor Maat.

It seemed like a foolish question, but Atharva had no readily available answer. Of course, he *wanted* to open it, but *should* he? In time, the hatch would undoubtedly be opened, but the more pertinent question was: should they open it now?

'We should wait,' he said at last. 'Bring in specialised cutting equipment. Stasis capsules, hermetic vault-chests and pressure suits. We can have no contamination of the site.'

He sensed Hathor Maat's impatience and looked back up the shaft. Niko Ashkali's head and shoulders were silhouetted in a square of light high above. The magna-storm and seismic activity had made the stairs bolted to the walls of the shaft too dangerous to use, so, much to her chagrin, she was forced to watch the Thousand Sons drop down until the safety of what lay below could be established.

'Wait?' said Hathor Maat. 'In case you hadn't noticed, this planet is on a countdown to extinction.'

'I know that, but if we are reckless we risk losing everything this ship may teach us of Morningstar's past.'

'And if we hesitate, we could lose it anyway. It's calm just now, but who knows how long that will last? Come on, Atharva, we *have* to open it!'

'Do not pretend your desire to open this is in service of future posterity,' said Atharva. 'You just want to be the first to uncover what lies within.'

'Don't you?'

Atharva had to admit he was tempted to give way before Hathor Maat's insistence. To be the discoverer of a relic from before Old Night, from the Golden Age of Exploration itself, would be a great honour.

A distant tremor rocked the ground. Dust and steel pipework fell into the shaft.

'Come on, Atharva,' said Hathor Maat. 'Who knows how long this place will last? We have to go in.'

Though he was loath to proceed without the proper protocols and equipment in place, Atharva knew they had no choice.

'Very well,' he said at last. 'We will open it.'

They both took hold of the locking bar, its metal smooth and cold to the touch. The edges of the hatch had been welded shut, the line of the seam ragged and uneven, as though done in great haste.

Atharva flexed his fingers on the bar, an artefact that had been forged thousands of years ago by men who knew nothing of the great expansion their efforts would precede.

A moment such as this ought to be savoured.

'Ready?' said Hathor Maat.

'I am,' replied Atharva, and despite his dislike of the legionary, he was elated like a neophyte on his first excavation.

'Pull!' said Hathor Maat.

They hauled the locking bar, and legionary strength and psychic power vied with the resistance of the welded seam in a one-sided battle. Atharva's Pyrae focus weakened the fusion bonds of the weld, as Hathor Maat altered his biochemistry and muscle density to exert greater power. The seam gave way moments later, cracking where the locking bolts would sit.

A sulphurous breath of pressurised air vented from the opening as they swung the hatch wide on protesting hinges. A groaning sound, as of ancient metal settling, echoed from deep within the starship.

'I am a fool,' said Atharva, instantly wary. 'This is no relic, and this is no excavation site.'

'What do you mean?'

He pointed to the exposed lock mechanisms of the hatch.

'Someone was in a great hurry to seal this hatch behind them. Why? The air inside is under pressure, which means this place still has power.'

'Why would someone do that?' said Hathor Maat.

'I do not know,' said Atharva. 'But let us think logically. The presence of this shaft and the structure overhead tells me that someone discovered this ship long ago. They must have already explored it, but why seal the hatch?'

'Maybe they finished their exploration?'

'Even so, why weld the hatch shut?'

'Contamination?'

'Perhaps, but it is probably safe to assume that any pathogens within will be long dead.'

Hathor Maat laughed, picking up on Atharva's enthusiasm for exploration. 'You want to go in as much as I do, don't you?'

'Yes,' admitted Atharva.

'Well, now we *definitely* need to get inside.'

SIX

LEVIATHAN RISES • IDLE HANDS • HAMMER OF THE GODS

Tensions were high in Calaena's orbital command centre. The moment Vashti had been planning for the last six days had finally arrived. She chewed the inside of her mouth, glanding a mixture of stimms and mood-stabilisers almost non-stop as the plates of the windows vibrated with powerful gravitic waves from the landing fields.

'Come on, come on, come on...' she muttered under her breath for the tenth time in the last two minutes. 'Lift, damn you, lift.'

The monster of steel that was the subject of her imprecations sat in a haze of distortion, making it difficult to see whether or not her words were having any effect.

'A little respect might help,' offered Magos Rom from the centre of her entoptic sphere of data light. 'The Machine knows all. The Machine *hears* all.'

'Fine,' snapped Vashti. 'Lift, damn you, lift. *Please.*'

'Not quite what I had in mind, but it will have to do.'

'It's all I've got, Tessza,' said Vashti.

Her every nerve and sinew was bowstring-taut. All of her staff were fixated on their data-slates, watching for signs of trouble in the launch. Tens of thousands of vital elements needed to go right for the *Lux Ferem* to get off the ground, and only one had to go wrong for the launch to fail.

Then… *it happened*. The ship and the ground parted company.

The console nearest her chirruped, indicating sufficient height had been gained to engage the platform repulsors.

'Yes,' said Vashti. 'Kick the platforms to negative four-gee, increasing to ten-gee in twenty-second increments.'

She glanced over at the tension ratio in the tug cables.

'Increase thrust on the tugs four points. They need to lift smooth as glass or they'll tear loose.'

'Yes, commander,' said Korinna Moreno, transmitting the order from her station by flicking a series of a mother-of-pearl switches. 'Order sent.'

'Airspace clear?'

'Clear,' answered Moreno and an exhausted cheer went up. Hands were shaken, backs were slapped and tearful embraces given. Vashti smiled and her chin sank to her chest as she let out a relieved breath. She wiped the back of her hand over her forehead.

'Right, people,' she said. 'I want everyone to stay sharp – we're not done yet. This old girl's just stretched her wings, but we still need to see her all the way.'

The chatter died down a little and Vashti walked to the edge of the command centre, peering down onto the platforms through the vibrating armourglass.

No matter how many times she laid eyes on it, the colossal scale of the *Lux Ferem* still defied comprehension. The hard vacuum of the void was this vessel's natural home, not the crushing gravity of a planet. Though she knew it was possible and – according to her command centre's instruments – was actually happening, common sense told Vashti it should be impossible for something of such inhuman scale to achieve escape velocity.

And yet it had. She could see it right in front of her.

Vashti laughed in delight and hammered a fist on the glass. 'Yes, damn it! You're actually flying, you beautiful girl!'

A shadow was forming beneath the colossal starship, a black footprint on Morningstar's surface, with radiating lines from the tug fleet helping to drag the ship's unimaginable mass into the sky. Under normal circumstances, the *Lux Ferem*'s engines would be fully capable of lifting it into orbit, but with every hold packed to the gunwales with evacuees and supplies to keep them alive, the old girl needed a little help.

Vashti's eyes drifted from the rising leviathan to the hordes of frightened people still waiting behind lines of demarcation and strategically deployed groups of Space Marines. An augmetic implant in her right eye did a swift calculation based on how many people they'd managed to get away and how many remained. She factored in projected loading times, number of civilian ships available and the Magos Geologicus' best estimate of the time Morningstar had left.

She came up short, and her delight at the *Lux Ferem*'s imminent departure evaporated. She didn't have enough ships to carry everyone to safety.

'So many people are going to be left behind,' she said.

She remembered the briefing where the grim-faced titan who led the Iron Warriors had spoken of the unavoidable loss of life the evacuation would incur. He spoke as if people were simply statistics, but by the end of his briefing – even through his stoically logical facade – she felt his genuine regret. Vashti told herself she could deal with it. They couldn't save everyone.

Saving some was better than saving none.

But seeing just how many would never escape Morningstar, she wasn't sure she could ever forgive herself for leaving them to die.

Could anyone?

* * *

The heavily laden Stormbird followed the coast northwards towards Calaena, keeping beneath clashing atmospherics that, more and more, were sounding like screaming. Morningstar was entering its last days and howled its pain on the wind.

Magnus tried to shut it out, but even with his eye closed and his senses blunted, he could still hear the psychic echoes of the world's doom. His flesh shimmered with heat as the alchemy wrought by the Emperor's gene-wrights worked miracles within his flesh to renew him. The damage was extensive, more than he had ever suffered before, so he tried to hang on to how it felt.

More than that, he still carried the immense power he had drawn from Morningstar's volatile heart. It simmered just beneath his skin, potent and seething with the desire to be unleashed. He kept it locked within, chained like suppressed rage or a buried secret. Such power needed to be released slowly, like a deep-sea diver decompressing on his way to the surface.

The process would be painful, agonisingly so, but Magnus had borne worse before and endured. Teeth gritted against the repercussive pain filling his bones with broken glass, he let his gaze roam the Stormbird's interior.

A hundred or more bloodied survivors pulled from the wreckage of Attar packed the troop compartment alongside weary, dust-covered legionaries. Mortal and transhuman sat side by side on bulkhead benches or slumped upon the swaying deck plates, their auras sapped of vitality.

His warriors had driven themselves to the very edge of their abilities in Attar, employing every aspect to save as many of its people as they could. Every one of them would be changed by what they had seen and done.

Magnus had never been more proud of his sons than now.

To see such devastation and to take in such innocence lost

was difficult for all of them, Magnus especially. His sons were suffering and he could not help them. Not this time.

Helplessness was anathema to him. When he had last felt this way he had made a decision he always knew might haunt him in years to come. Today was not that day, but seeing his sons bloodied and all but broken sent a tremor of unease through his furnace-hot body.

He opened his eye as the sound of roaring engines screamed past the Stormbird. From the tone and pitch, he identified promethium-based ramjets, most likely a Primaris Thunderbolt fighter squadron. An escort for the governor, perhaps, or additional protection despatched by Perturabo?

Neither, it seemed, for the jets roared onwards to Calaena.

Magnus glanced towards the rear of the Stormbird's troop compartment, where Konrad Vargha was being treated. The man was weeping and incoherent with pain. His legs were extensively damaged, but thanks to Magnus' intervention, he would likely keep them. The governor's survival was miraculous, and while it had been brave of him to venture out into Attar, his duty was in Calaena, putting a human face on the sacrifices necessary to save as many of Morningstar's inhabitants as possible.

But Magnus could not fault a leader willing to dirty his hands in order to save those he loved.

Ahriman barged through the crowds, pushing his senses into the throng of refugees. He had not the time for simply skimming thoughts. Instead he punched through the flimsy mental barriers mortals wove around their minds, which they believed impervious.

Everyone who met his gaze fell back, crying out as he tore into their thoughts for signs of the treachery he had seen. Men and women dropped to their knees, screaming and clutching their skulls in pain.

Who will it be? From where will they strike?

He pushed deep into the crowds, scattering them like herd animals with an apex predator in their midst. He spread his psychic net wide, seeking one path among millions that might lead to the vision he had seen, a fleeting trace of future echoes in the thoughts of tens of thousands.

'Where are you?' he muttered.

Forrix followed him through the crowds, bolter ready to take out any threat the instant it was revealed to him.

'Anything?' he demanded. 'Give me a target.'

'I don't have one.'

'Find one.'

'One mind among so many...' said Ahriman, taking deep breaths, but trying to calm himself in the face of such desperation was all but impossible.

'It will not be one mind,' said Forrix.

'What?'

'What you saw – it will not be one mind, it will be many.'

'How can you know that?' said Ahriman, turning on the spot.

'What you described was too devastating and too complex for one person. There will be others helping whoever is going to do this. Seek connections and you will find them.'

Ahriman took a calming breath, using the cantrips of the lower Enumerations to balance his humours. Forrix was right: an operation of this magnitude would take numerous individuals to execute, with many moving parts and traitors within the very institutions set up to protect these civilians.

The scale of such treachery was hard to fathom.

He nodded and curled his fingertips together, one palm above the other.

'Seek not the psychneuein,' he said. 'Follow the threads of its mind web, and you will be led to the host.'

'What's that?'

'An old cautionary tale of Prospero,' said Ahriman, turning to face Forrix. He put a hand on the Iron Warrior's shoulder guard and looked him square in the eye.

'I need you to watch over me, Forrix,' he said.

'What do you mean?'

'To do what I need to do, I need to detach an element of my psychic awareness. My consciousness will be... elsewhere. That will leave my body vulnerable, so I ask that you protect it.'

'I don't know exactly what that means, but I swear no harm will come to you while I watch over you,' promised Forrix.

'Thank you, my friend,' said Ahriman. 'You honour me.'

'Go,' said Forrix. 'Find them and stop them.'

Ahriman nodded, then let slip the bindings of flesh and soared into the sky.

Perhaps a hundred metres of clear air separated the *Lux Ferem* from the ground. Vashti was trying not to hold her breath as it climbed. Every metre from the surface was a victory that saw every life aboard it closer to safety. Its vast bulk shivered like a newborn taking its first steps. The glowing repulsor plates on its belly were hazed with building energy.

'Altitude?' she asked, unable to take her eyes from the struggling vessel.

'One hundred and sixty metres,' said Korinna Moreno. 'Rising at a rate of ten metres a second.'

'Come on,' said Vashti, chewing her bottom lip and running the numbers in her head. Tessza Rom beat her to it.

'The *Lux Ferem* needs at least five hundred metres of clear air before she can safely engage her ventral repulsors,' said Magos Rom.

'I know that, Tessza,' said Vashti.

'And even that is much lower than I would recommend.'

'Two hundred metres,' said Moreno. 'High enough.'

Before Vashti could correct Moreno, the noospheric globe of light around Tessza Rom flickered an ugly red as eight unauthorised contacts entered her tightly controlled airspace.

'Who the hell…?' Vashti said, turning her attention to the icons flickering to life at the edge of her panel.

'Fast movers,' said Rom. 'Coming in from the south. Transponders identify them as a Primaris squadron. Thunderbolts, previously based in Attar.'

'What the hell are they doing here?' swore Vashti. 'I don't have space for a drop pod, let alone a whole squadron of cocksure aviators. Vox the squadron lead and tell him to get out of my airspace!'

'I am trying,' said Tessza, data light swirling around her station. 'No reply.'

'Throne, are they blind or just stupid?' said Vashti. 'Attar might be gone, but I don't have space to land a jetbike here.'

She snatched up the vox-horn and dialled into the frequency displayed on the transponder read-outs.

'Primaris Lead, be advised you are entering a highly volatile, controlled airspace,' she said, struggling to remain calm even as she watched the icons of the fighters drawing closer. 'Alter your heading immediately. Do not approach the exclusion zone around Calaena space port. You are *not* cleared to enter, and I am authorised to employ deadly force to keep my airspace just the way I want it.'

Static was her only answer. The Thunderbolts kept coming, so she pressed the vox-switch again.

'Thunderbolts Primaris, I say again, alter your heading immediately. A boundary line of of three kilometres exists around this location. If you violate that you *will* be fired upon. This is your final warning.'

The vox crackled with connection static.

'Finally,' said Vashti.

'*Hail Shaitan!*' said Primaris Lead.

'What was that?' said Vashti. 'Say again, Primaris Lead?'

'He said, "Hail Shaitan",' said Korinna Moreno, standing and disconnecting from her cogitator bank as if leaving at the end of a work rotation.

'What are you doing, Korinna?' said Vashti. 'Link back into your station.'

Moreno did not answer. Instead, she spread wide her arms.

Her porcelain-smooth augmetic limb unfolded with machine precision to reveal wads of tightly packed fyceline. In her other hand, she held a detonator.

'Korinna, what–' began Vashti.

'Hail Shaitan!' said Moreno, pressing the detonator's trigger.

In a blazing explosion of white fire and fury, Calaena's orbital command centre went dark.

Forrix had no clear idea what to expect, but he knew the exact moment Ahriman's presence left his body. The legionary of the Thousand Sons went stiff, his muscles locking him in position. Panicked crowds milled in confusion, shrouded in the shadow of the mighty starship as it fought for altitude. The ordered columns in which they had been made to march through the city were broken, and frightened faces looked to him for direction.

'Get down on your knees,' said Forrix, knowing that keeping people static was likely the best option for now. 'And stay down until an Iron Warrior tells you to get back up.'

Those people nearest to him complied instantly. The rest followed suit in concentric waves, making Forrix feel like he stood at the epicentre of their devotion. The notion briefly amused him until the ever-widening circle of kneeling refugees revealed an approaching column of Army vehicles that had no business being this close to the loading zones.

Four Praetors and two Hydra flak tanks.

The presence of such armoured vehicles within the precincts of a space port was entirely normal; each was specifically designed to engage aerial enemies. But such mobile artillery was usually deployed towards the perimeter of a defended zone.

The anti-aircraft tanks ground to a halt, and Forrix's unease grew as he watched their crews begin bracing protocols.

In readiness to fire.

He looked to Ahriman's immobile body. Could the legionary be lifted or would that break whatever trance he was in?

Forrix had no way of knowing, but bent to sling Ahriman onto his shoulder. The warrior was a dead weight across him, loose-limbed like a casualty.

Forrix set off at a jog through the kneeling multitudes towards the tanks. He held Ahriman tight over one shoulder, his bolter held low beside his leg. The soldiers working on the tanks saw him coming and their reaction told Forrix everything he needed to know about their intent.

'Legionary Forrix to all Iron Warrior units. Enemy in the wire. I repeat, enemy in the wire. Until further notice, treat all local Red Dragon and Army forces as enemy combatants.'

He couldn't know for sure that every Morningstar soldier was hostile, but the Iron Warriors operated a zero-uncertainty policy within their perimeters.

'Enemy anti-aircraft units are in position to attack the *Lux Ferem*. Heavy support to my location immediately!'

A Praetor tank slowly turned on grinding tracks, bringing its heavy bolters to bear. Its crew formed a disciplined fireline.

Battle protocols. Think and move.

A flurry of las-bolts slashed towards Forrix. Paltry impacts blistered his armour. He ignored them; his Mark IV plate had been forged to withstand the worst the galaxy could throw at him.

A few shots hit Ahriman. More flayed the kneeling refugees. They screamed in terror and pressed themselves flat to the ground. Others died as they fled, cut down without mercy by the indiscriminate fire.

His anger built, inferno-hot.

Use it. Direct it.

Forrix raised his bolter. Targeting reticules centred on five soldiers.

Five dead men.

He fired one-handed, squeezing the trigger in smooth intervals. Genhanced flesh worked with his armour's servo-assisted muscles to dissipate recoil. Mass-reactive bolts blasted every target to blossoming sprays of pulped flesh and blood.

Now they'll run.

But in defiance of all Forrix had learned of transhuman dread, the others soldiers rushed him. They fired from the hip, screaming obscenities as they charged.

'You crave death?' he said. 'I am happy to oblige.'

He fired a stream of shells, cutting his attackers down in a blitzing storm of bolter fire. Not one survived to reach him.

Keep moving. Find cover before those tanks engage.

The unmistakable clatter of cycling auto-loaders sounded.

Too late.

Forrix dropped to one knee as the Praetor opened fire.

Heavy bolter. High-calibre mass-reactives.

Explosions ripped up the honeycombed structure of the landing platform in a line towards him, bolt shells chewing through screaming civilians. Plumes of metal-laced plascrete flew. Blood misted the air as bodies detonated. Forrix jinked right. Two shells clipped his left shoulder. Another hit him dead centre on his breastplate. The explosion rocked him back onto his haunches.

Find cover. Feel the iron within.

Forrix leaned into the fire, keeping his own bulk between the gunfire and Ahriman's supine body.

Another two shells detonated against his shoulder guard.

Warning icons bloomed to life on his visor.

Find cover!

Forrix surged to his feet and ran towards the largest concentration of bloodied bodies. He mag-locked his bolter to his thigh and scooped up four limp corpses, holding them close as the tank's gunner fired another salvo.

Shells ripped into his meat shields and the bodies convulsed under the impacts, acting as ablatives to detonate the mass-reactive warheads before they struck him. Blood sheeted his war-plate and bone fragments lodged in the cracks in his ceramite.

A Hydra tank moved into an enfilading position, its long-barrelled guns slowly rising to their engagement angle.

Burdened as he was, Forrix knew he wouldn't reach the Hydra before its guns opened up. He made another quarter-turn to shield Ahriman from the incoming fire as its cupola-mounted heavy stubber opened fire. Its shells raked him, shredding what remained of the corpses and pounding his armour. His war-plate cracked and split at the weaker flex-joints. Blood drizzled the spaces within his armour.

Forrix staggered as a mass-reactive round shattered his left knee. A spike of white-hot pain shot through his leg as shrapnel ricocheted down his shin bone and blew out his ankle. Pain suppressors flooded his system, numbing the flesh around his wound as adrenal stimms surged. He kept going, feeling cracked bone grinding within the shredded meat of his foot.

He roared and blasted the gunner from the turret mount of the Hydra. His visor was awash with target icons, spiking vitals and damage indicators. More shells followed him, but the angle was too sharp now for the gunners.

A flurry of rockets streaked from the other Praetors.

'Throne, no!' yelled Forrix as they slashed towards the *Lux Ferem*.

Ahriman soared into the sky, a comet unleashed from its earthly prison. His subtle body blazed with light, all the potential of his being coalesced into a glittering shooting star that craved the heavens once more.

The ground fell away, a terrestrial prison for corporeal form. The lightness of being was intoxicating, a sense of freedom beyond compare. As always, he fought the desire to never return to flesh, to exist in this perfect form of expression for all time.

This was the trap of the subtle body, a rush of sensation that some neophytes failed to master. They would soar on psychic zephyrs, freed from the banal necessities of existence and heedless of their body's disintegration. Only its eventual death severed the silver cord and dissipated their essence.

Ahriman flew in a curving arc around the gargantuan form of the *Lux Ferem*. Its structure was barely visible as a shadowed skeleton, like a vast void-swimming colossus whose belly was filled with wriggling prey. Tens of thousands of souls glimmered within the ship: frightened souls, grateful souls, spiteful souls and every other emotion running the gamut of human experience.

But chief among the emotions he felt was hope.

Humanity's greatest virtue, and its greatest weakness...

The heavy gravitic tugs were smudges of blunted emotion, cauterised wells of life without thoughts or feelings. The frontal lobes of their servitor pilots had been burned out, and Ahriman was revolted by such crude surgeries.

A ferocious spike of emotion drew his attention from the tugs, and he arced over in time to see the tower of the space port's orbital command centre vanish in a sheeting fireball. He felt echoes of horror, anger and righteous zeal bloom from the detonation.

Rapture...

Forrix was correct. Betrayals of this magnitude stretched beyond lone madmen or a few crazed adherents of a suppressed cult. This treachery ran deep.

Ahriman flinched as he felt a surge of that same rapture he had experienced in his vision below. He rolled in the air, soaring over the back of the iron leviathan struggling to reach the safety of the void, a journey that now seemed all but impossible.

One of lifter-tugs exploded in a cherry-red fireball, the detonation of its gravitic engine sending out an expanding wave of force. Another followed swiftly, falling onto the back of the *Lux Ferem* and smashing to pieces.

Ahriman saw the source of the destruction.

A flight of eight Thunderbolt fighters streaked towards the mass-conveyer with lethal intent. Streaks of fire blazed from underslung nose-cannons, while white contrails followed skystrike missiles as they leapt from wing pylons. Four more tugs exploded, easy prey for the heavy fighters.

The flight broke up, four peeling off to starboard, four to port. Guns chattering, they raked the flanks of the *Lux Ferem*. Alternating punches of autocannon and lascannon fire chewed up hull plates and tore away plasma thrusters and warp vanes.

Ahriman followed the starboard flight down. He rammed his consciousness into the mind of the trailing pilot. He felt the man's exhilaration, his desire to bring death to the thousands of people aboard the *Lux Ferem*. Ahriman vaporised his brain with a thought and the aircraft dropped out of formation, spinning out of control to the ground.

The remaining three craft scattered, believing they were under conventional attack. Ahriman stretched out his kine powers and slammed two aircraft together. They exploded as their unexpended ordnance detonated at the ferocious impact. The final aircraft spun in ever more desperate evasive manoeuvres, its pilot trying in vain to pinpoint the source of his comrades' demise.

Ahriman swooped low over the back of the corkscrewing aircraft and thrust his consciousness into the pilot's mind. He pressed the man's screaming thoughts hard against the lid of his skull, knowing in an instant every aspect of commanding this aerial steed.

He threw the plane into a steep climb, angling the winds to catch the thermals lifting off the back of the mass-conveyor. A fierce exhilaration filled him, and he understood a measure of the arrogance he saw in the swagger of every aviator he had ever met. Like the cavalrymen of Old Earth, the pilot of a combat aircraft was a god of the battlefield.

Ahriman rolled the Thunderbolt around, seeing the other four fighters looping back around for another strafing run. The air above the vast starship was smudged with explosions and drifting smoke from the downed tugs. The wreckage of at least a dozen burned on the *Lux Ferem*'s dorsal surfaces. Another salvo of missiles leapt from the wing hardpoints of the attacking fighters. They raced towards their targets, but at the last second, Ahriman twisted their course and turned them back upon their source.

There was something the Emperor had said on the day of His departure from Prospero. It seemed appropriate now.

The hawk always returns to the hand that loosed it...

Two Thunderbolts exploded as their own missiles flew into

their engine intakes. A third dropped out of the sky as Ahriman extended his powers and ripped its wings off like a child tormenting a trapped insect.

The final aircraft turned into him, its prow guns blazing. Ahriman vacated the pilot's mind as a hurricane of autocannon rounds shredded his Thunderbolt. The shock wave of its demise chased Ahriman, and his Pyrae powers ignited the air within the last Thunderbolt's cockpit.

He relished the pilot's agonised screams as he was burned alive in the raging firestorm within his aircraft. The fighter spun out and crashed in a tumbling fireball along the *Lux Ferem*'s upper surfaces.

Ahriman twisted in the air, his subtle body resonating with the power of the Great Ocean and the impunity with which he had destroyed these men. He searched for other aircraft, almost wishing there were more.

Then he saw it wouldn't matter.

As fast as he had killed the attacking fighters, it hadn't been fast enough.

More than half of the lifter-tugs had been destroyed.

The *Lux Ferem* was going down.

Forrix roared in anger as yet more blossoming explosions marched along the belly of the mass-conveyor. One of its repulsor generators blew out with a thunderous detonation. The shock wave buckled the air and drove anyone below who wasn't already there onto the ground.

More explosions erupted on the mass-conveyor's flanks, and shattered plating fell in a burning rain from the breached hull of the enormous vessel. An explosion mushroomed a few hundred metres away. Wreckage spun away from whatever had smashed into the ground.

Forrix saw a pair of raptor-winged interceptors streak

overhead. One vanished in a tumbling fireball as the pursuing aircraft's guns blew out its engines. He didn't have time to wonder what was going on overhead.

Get up. Keep moving.

'From iron cometh strength,' said Forrix through gritted teeth. 'From strength cometh will.'

Pushing past the agony of his shattered knee, he surged to his feet and limped towards the nearest Hydra. Every step brought pain, but he had to keep going. Another crewman climbed to the Hydra's cupola mount and threw his dead comrade from the vehicle. Forrix blasted him from the vehicle's topside with a single shot. The slide racked back empty.

No time to reload.

'From will cometh faith. From faith cometh honour.'

Another salvo of missiles leapt from the Praetors' launchers, detonating moments later against the *Lux Ferem*'s hull. More wreckage tumbled downwards as the explosions blew out the bulkheads of cargo holds, and Forrix saw flailing bodies tumbling from the ruptured starship. Even over the bellow of gunfire and the bone-shaking bass note of the *Lux Ferem*'s struggling repulsors, Forrix heard their terrified screams.

He reached the forward hull of the Hydra and bent his one good leg before pistoning upwards. He landed on the tank's topside. His ruined knee shrieked and a veil of blinding agony fell across his vision. A crewman emerged from the cupola, holding a crackling volkite caliver. Forrix smashed his bolter down on the soldier's skull, crushing bone and helmet to shards.

'From honour cometh iron.'

The Hydra's guns were angled up towards the *Lux Ferem*, the turret rotated to the side. The two gunners looked around in surprise at the sight of this blood-soaked giant lumbering towards them. Their surprise did not last long. Forrix killed both with sweeps of his bolter, using the weapon like a club. He kicked their bodies from the crew platform and laid Ahriman down as gently as possible against the rear handrail.

A flurry of shots spanked from the blast shield around the wide barrels of the upraised autocannons. He ducked into cover as a searing-hot beam of plasma exploded against the shield, turning its upper quadrant to molten slag.

The workings of a Hydra were no mystery to Forrix; an Iron Warrior could operate any artillery piece in the Imperial armoury. He pressed himself into the contoured shoulder grips, squatting to fit his armoured bulk in a space designed for mortal frames. He stamped the pivot pedal and swung the quad-barrelled weapon around as more gunfire impacted the hissing blast shield: las-fire and plasma bolts, along with heavy slugs and missiles from bipod-mounted launchers.

Red-hot fragments ricocheted around him, perforating his shoulder and neck.

He ignored them and centred the Praetor in the Hydra's sights.

'This is my Unbreakable Litany. May it forever be so,' said Forrix, squeezing the palm-triggers.

The Hydra bucked like a wild bull-grox. The noise was deafening, like the very fabric of the world being ripped asunder. All four barrels unleashed a blizzard of high-explosive shells into the nearest Praetor's flank. The vehicle vanished in a blinding fireball as the rockets inside cooked off in a series of booming detonations.

But his triumph was short-lived as he saw it had come too late, that Ahriman's apocalyptic vision was coming to pass.

The *Lux Ferem* was going down.

It fell back to Morningstar with infinite grace, but Forrix knew that something of such titanic mass would cause untold devastation upon impact.

He turned from the slowly falling starship, seeing a hundred or more red-armoured soldiers advancing on his captured Hydra. Many were armed with weapons easily capable of taking out his newly acquired tank. Not that it mattered now.

He swung the turret around, lowering the quad-mounted autocannons as far as they could go.

'Iron within, iron without,' he said.

SEVEN

EVEN IN DEATH • MATTERS THEOSOPHICAL • A GOD FALLS

Returning to flesh was never easy.

Like a slave freed of its fetters and then forced back into servitude by a trusted friend, the spirit felt betrayal as its cage of meat and bone enfolded it once more. Its vengeance was repercussive pain, a bone-deep ache and weariness that took longer to fade the farther and freer the soul had flown.

Ahriman awoke in an acrid, chemical-rich fog.

He blinked away after-images of exploding fighter jets and reached up to run a hand over his face. His palm came away bloody.

When had he removed his helmet?

It lay beside him, scorched and torn by impacts.

Where was he?

A rush of sensory information came to him. Metal railings, the stench of blood and the acrid reek of propellant gases. Fyceline and lapping powder. He heard thousands of screaming voices and a deep, rumbling vibration that felt like the beginnings of a world-shattering earthquake.

He was propped up against the crew barrier of a mobile artillery piece, a Hydra by the looks of it, its barrels bleeding heat

123

and drooling smoke, its breech buckled and spewing fumes both toxic and flammable.

Slumped before him was a figure he only recognised as Forrix due to the configuration of his aura. The Iron Warrior's armour was all but gone, the ceramite plates fused with his flesh and running like wax across his body. His skin was roasted black with vapour flash and what looked like plasma burns or melta flare. His breathing was the ragged, embattled hikes of collapsing lungs.

Forrix lifted his head, and Ahriman saw one eye was a fused, milky-white of burn tissue. The other swam with incomprehension before recognition set in.

'Ahriman...' wheezed Forrix. 'Apologies. I swore no harm would come to you while I watched over you.'

Ahriman pushed himself to his feet and swept his gaze around him. The Hydra was a steel island amid a sea of corpses. At least two hundred bodies surrounded it, each one clad in the red livery of Morningstar. He read the scene in an instant, knowing Forrix had killed them all in defence of him and this solitary bastion.

'You kept me alive, my friend,' said Ahriman, kneeling by Forrix and placing a palm on his ruined chest. The Iron Warrior flinched, his every nerve on fire. Ahriman reached deep inside himself and used his Pavoni arts to blunt Forrix's pain. It was the least he could do to ease the man's passage into death.

Forrix shook his head and clamped a fused fist around Ahriman's gauntlet.

'No,' he said. 'A legionary of the Fourth... never... turns from pain.'

'Not even in death?'

'Especially not... then,' said Forrix, tilting his head to look into the sky. 'Anyway, you would be... wasting... your powers.'

Ahriman looked up just as the drifting clouds of propellant

parted, pushed aside by clashing gravitic waves to reveal the blasted underside of the *Lux Ferem*. A drizzle of torn metal fell from the mass-conveyor's belly as it sank back to the ground.

A sick sense of inevitability settled in Ahriman's gut.

'This is what I saw,' he said. 'This is how it ends.'

'In fire... and blood,' said Forrix. 'As... it should be. For warriors... like us...'

In a matter of minutes, Calaena would be obliterated.

Perturabo and his senior officers stood upon the highest bastion of the Sharei Maveth, watching helplessly as the *Lux Ferem* fell from the sky. Perturabo gripped the edge of the parapet with force enough to crumble its stonework.

They had watched in horror as anti-aircraft ordnance had raked the belly of the mass-conveyor and raged impotently as an entire squadron of Thunderbolts blasted the gravitic tugs from the sky.

Those same fighters had, one by one, destroyed themselves in an inexplicable paroxysm of self-immolation. His warriors had speculated on a schism within the traitors' ranks, but Perturabo alone had seen the faintest nimbus of something incorporeal streaking between the fighters before each explosion.

There could be only one explanation.

'That is the work of the Thousand Sons,' he whispered.

'My lord?' said Barban Falk. 'The Fifteenth caused this?'

'No,' said Perturabo. 'They are trying to stop it.'

'What is about to happen is beyond anyone's power to stop.'

Perturabo did not reply, knowing that Falk was entirely correct.

Thousands of refugees were fleeing in panic through Calaena's streets. Others stood in enraptured horror, staring up at their doom as it fell from the sky. But stand or run, none of them would survive the mass-conveyor's impact. The faint sound of terrified screams was carried on the winds blowing in off the ocean.

The *Lux Ferem* shuddered like a wounded beast as its captain fought a futile battle to keep it aloft. Glittering debris rained from its wounded flanks.

'Come on,' urged Harkor, staring at the ship and slamming a fist on the parapet. 'Fight, damn you. Keep her in the air!'

Barban Falk shook his head. 'An impossible task, Harkor. When that ship hits, everyone in the city is going to die. The Sons of Shaitan have been thorough in their betrayal.'

'Faithless cowards,' said Harkor. 'Their treachery has condemned tens of thousands.'

Hot anger surged through Perturabo at Harkor's words, a primal fury that roared with the need to hit back at those responsible for this atrocity.

'That is the least of their sins,' said Perturabo. 'They have broken their oath of loyalty to the Emperor. That oath is an inviolable covenant, one that can never be reforged once broken. For such betrayers there can be no forgiveness, only the most painful of deaths.'

Perturabo looked away from the doomed starship, feeling himself inexorably drawn to look up at the malignant sky. Vivid magna-storms burned in the upper atmosphere, hurling spears of lightning to the planet's surface and painting the line of the horizon with electric fire.

Even through the nightmarish storms, Perturabo – and Perturabo alone – could still see the distant star-maelstrom, its unnatural energies swirling like a whirlpool in a stagnant ocean. It stared down at him like the eye of a patient hunter, as it had since he had first seen it clinging to the rain-soaked cliffs of Lochos.

Were its energies brighter around Morningstar?

He tore his gaze from the heavens, his mind racing to calculate the likely force and radius of the *Lux Ferem*'s impact.

Calaena would be destroyed, that much was certain.

The Sharei Maveth would suffer severe damage, yes, but it would endure. He briefly considered opening the gates to those civilians near enough to reach them, but almost immediately rejected the notion. How could he be certain he would not be admitting the same traitors who had brought down the *Lux Ferem*?

With a heavy heart, Perturabo knew only one logical course of action was open to him.

'Pull every warrior within the Sharei Maveth,' he said. 'We batten down the hatches. I want every gate sealed, every portal locked and every blast shield engaged. And power up the void generators. I think we're going to need them.'

He turned away from the coming catastrophe.

The evacuation was in ruins, but Perturabo's mind now turned to ways it might yet be salvaged. If Magos Tancorix's calculations were correct, time remained to construct temporary landing fields on the plains around Zharrukin. They were wide enough to bring trans-atmospheric troop-ships down from the orbiting fleets. It would be a fraction of how many they could have saved, but–

'Throne!' yelled Barban Falk, pointing at something over the parapet. 'Coming in from the south. What is he thinking?'

Perturabo snapped from his calculations and looked to where Falk had indicated. He saw a lightning-struck Stormbird arcing in over the coastline. Its engines were on fire and it was heading straight to the heart of the landing platforms, as if seeking to join the vast bulk of the *Lux Ferem* in death.

The Stormbird's hull rippled along its length with burning fuel and it shuddered as it passed through the tortured magnetic fields surrounding the *Lux Ferem*.

He knew instantly who was on board.

'What is that pilot doing?' asked Harkor. 'Is he insane?'

'Perhaps,' said Perturabo. 'It's Magnus.'

* * *

Curiously, Ahriman felt little fear as the vastness of the *Lux Ferem* closed in, a crushing sky falling to end him and everyone in Calaena. He eased his mind into the third Enumeration, finding solace in the clarity it brought.

If this is death, then it is not so terrible.

He looked over at Forrix, his flesh burned to the bone, and reconsidered that thought. Blood pulsed from the Iron Warrior's many wounds, grievous hurts even transhuman biology could not undo.

Despite Forrix's wishes, Ahriman turned his power upon him. He subtly closed the pain gates in the Iron Warrior's spine, hearing a groan of relief escape his scorched lips.

'This is what you saw?' asked Forrix.

Ahriman nodded. 'Yes.'

'And do such visions always come to pass?'

'Most of the time.'

'Only *most*?'

'Sometimes, by knowing the future, you can change it.'

'The implication being that you never actually saw the future, merely a *potential* future, yes?'

Ahriman smiled. 'I underestimated you, Forrix.'

'Most people do, but am I correct?'

'I cannot give you a definitive answer, my friend,' said Ahriman. 'We hold conclaves within the Fellowships that seek to answer such questions, but none have yet found a satisfactory answer.'

'I have one,' said Forrix.

'You can answer a riddle that has confounded the greatest thinkers of the Thousand Sons?'

'There's that arrogance again.'

'Apologies.'

Forrix shook his head. 'We have only a few moments left to live. Don't waste them asking for forgiveness.'

'Then tell me your answer so I do not die in ignorance.'

'Very well,' said Forrix. 'These visions you have? You see them and you act to thwart them or see them come to fruition.'

'Yes.'

'If everything you see is merely a potential future, then the very act of seeing it changes the outcome in one of two ways. First, if your vision is of, say, my death and it still comes to pass, no matter whether you let it happen or resisted it, then the future was set and nothing you could have done would have made any difference. Or, if by acting, you change it so I live, then was it truly a vision of the future? By seeing me die, did you change the future because you were then compelled to save me? So my question is this – are you changing the future by seeing it, or are potential futures changing you?'

Ahriman nodded, pleased at Forrix's insight, basic though it was. Did he truly believe the brightest minds of the Thousand Sons had not already debated this thought experiment a hundred times over?

'You pick a strange time for a discussion on matters theosophical, my friend,' said Ahriman.

'I don't often get the chance among the Fourth,' said Forrix. 'The Dodekatheon is a place of hard realities, not matters intangible.'

'The Dodekatheon?'

'One of our mason's lodges within the Legion,' said Forrix. 'A meeting place for builders and strategists to come together and test which of the newest theories of fortifications – their raising and razing, if you will – are in ascendence.'

Forrix looked up and Ahriman saw the acceptance of death in his one remaining eye. Perhaps there was something to the myths of Old Earth of surrendering an eye in return for wisdom after all.

'I wish I had more time to know you, Forrix,' said Ahriman.

'To learn of your Legion and its ways. I suspect there is a great deal we could teach one another.'

'If only we had more time,' said Forrix, 'but that is the one resource we can never recoup.'

'In the Great Ocean, all things are possible,' said Ahriman, holding out his hand.

Forrix took his wrist in the warrior's grip.

And a roaring tide of power surged through Ahriman. The scarab on his armour's chest-plate blazed with light, and he felt a connection between him and every single warrior of the Thousand Sons.

A red veil fell over Ahriman's eyes and he saw Forrix relentlessly marching across a bloody battlefield, the bones of millions ground to ash beneath his boots. The Iron Warrior was wreathed in the corrosion and dust of an unending war fought in the darkness of a far future.

Engulfed in storms of iron and fire, wading through blood and death with burning banners raised all around him, this Forrix was a monster.

'You live...' breathed Ahriman, his limbs swelling with power the likes of which he never imagined he might feel. 'You will not die on Morningstar.'

The vision of Forrix as a dark god beneath a black sun returned to him and he lowered his gaze towards the wounded Iron Warrior.

'But you must.'

Ahriman raised his arm, ready to kill Forrix where he lay, but cried out as yet more agony suffused his limbs.

This was dangerous, lethal power. The kind each flight in the Great Ocean promised in its hollow blandishments, but which every initiate was warned never to touch. It pulled him to his feet as if he were a puppet moved by the will of a cruel master. Fire blazed in his eyes as all his arts, in all their most potent forms, erupted from his flesh. Raptora energies warped the metal of the Hydra like softened wax. Athanaean insight revealed every banal secret within Forrix's single-minded skull.

The Iron Warrior howled in pain as Ahriman's Pavoni arts restored life to his flesh, remaking shattered bones, regenerating scraps of organs and slathering fresh-grown skin over previously scorched meat.

Corvidae prescience showed him Morningstar shattered, its core sundered, its air stripped away and the void echoing to the disbelieving screams of its people.

His neck snapped around as he felt the approach of something incredible, something brighter than a thousand stars – a psychic fire that could burn the entire world then work miracles with its ashes.

It came in like the phoenix of legend.

A Stormbird, its hull burning from prow to stern.

And standing upon its frontal assault ramp was a messianic figure of red fire, a cyclopean titan of unimaginable power and infinite majesty.

+Father,+ said Ahriman.

The dying steel leviathan filled the sky, its impossible length stretching to the horizon, a hammer of the gods come to smite the earth and bring about its ruination. Burning metal and screaming flesh fell from ruptured compartments. Men and women leapt to their deaths rather than be consumed by the fires raging within the starship's belly.

The power filling Magnus, the seismic force dragged from the heart of the planet, still raged within his breast. Any thoughts of ritual dissipation, of a gradual psychic decompression, were moot, for now he had the perfect release.

Phosis T'kar stood beside Magnus on the burning Stormbird's assault ramp, his aura ablaze with exhilaration and fear.

Will this work or has my arrogance sealed our fate?

'Can you *really* do this, my lord?' asked Phosis T'Kar, echoing the primarch's thought.

'I truly don't know,' said Magnus, moving through every one of the Enumerations to prepare for the impossible feat he was about to attempt. 'But nor can I simply leave the tens of thousands of people aboard the *Lux Ferem* and in Calaena to their doom.'

Phosis T'kar nodded, the decision made. 'Then what can I do?'

'You are already doing it.'

The scarab upon Phosis T'kar's chest had been hewn from the crystalline walls of the Reflecting Caves below Tizca and now served as a conduit between him and his gene-sire. Through these psychically resonant gemstones, Magnus could touch the soul of every one of his sons.

He felt as they felt, shouldering their every emotion.

He took on their indignant rage at what was being lost on Morningstar and shared their unquenchable thirst for new knowledge.

But most of all he shared their deep longing to reveal their true selves. Their powers were as much a part of them as breathing, and to keep that hidden from their brother Legions was to keep a part of their soul in chains.

From one son, Magnus felt the barely acknowledged fear that his primarch was leading them down into a darkness from which there could be no return. He knew who that was, of course. Magnus had known since their first meeting on Prospero, when he had tried to hide the agony he was suffering, that the future would set them on altogether different paths.

This intimate connection between Magnus and his sons allowed no secrets to be kept, no truths to be unacknowledged or desires hidden away.

The power was intoxicating.

To know *everything*. Who would not wish such a boon?

Their power and love flowed to him, augmented him, a thousand conduits to the Great Ocean. He took that energy and shaped it, wielding more power than any had before him.

Had the Emperor ever dared so greatly? Perhaps, but He rarely spoke of the full extent of His reach. Would Magnus be the first of the primarchs to eclipse their father's deeds?

Magnus tried to dismiss the thought as fleeting arrogance, but a thorn of it remained lodged in his heart. And who would blame him? What son did not aspire to be more than his father?

The Stormbird slammed down, skidding in an arcing loop across the platform. Promethium sprayed like rain from its ruptured tanks, instantly igniting in the flames burning along its wings.

The gunship bounced back into the air, before slamming down onto its belly and breaking its back. The landing gear shattered instantly, sheared away by the force of the impact. Orange sparks flared from grinding, shrieking metal. The Stormbird howled in pain as it finally ground to a halt, billowing smoke and flames.

Magnus leapt from the downed gunship and his warriors followed him without question. Their power flowed into him, honed and distilled by the scarab gems upon their breastplates.

The belly of the *Lux Ferem* was a hundred metres above them. *Ninety, eighty...*

Clashing electromagnetics from damaged repulsors churned the air. Coolant discharge vented from its colossal drive cores. Hurricane winds scoured the platform in localised tornadoes and burning plasma vortices. Every step onwards became a battle.

Magnus bent into the storm of gravitic waves and plasma fire, feeling his skin blister in the intolerable heat. His hair charred and crisped as his warriors formed the mandala around him, the paint bubbling and peeling on their war-plate.

Fifty metres...

Magnus looked up and thrust his arms to the sky with a word of change upon his lips. He unleashed the vast power roiling with him and let the world's wounded core pour through him. He channelled it, shaped it and bent it to his will. His sons added what little they could, their power infinitesimal next to the energies he sought to master.

Magnus drew upon his deepest raptures, formulae he had only ever read of in the Emperor's most secret vaults. Unchecked energies wrought him into a being of purest energy, a titan at the end of the world, the great god Donar wrestling the great World Serpent in the last great battle. Blinding waves of aetheric raptures poured from him in a thunderous bow wave as his power met the descending force of the *Lux Ferem*.

Could his body endure what was being demanded of it?

The underside of the vast starship crumpled as its weight pressed down on the psychic force pushing upwards.

Colossal bulkheads designed to withstand the push and pull of void manoeuvring and warp translation bent and split under stresses beyond their power to endure. Hull plates thick enough to withstand explosive ordnance peeled back like wet parchment. Hydraulic fluids drizzled and burned in the swirling flames.

Magnus roared, his mind expanding in a lattice of geometric progression. Every breath was fire in his lungs. He was driven down to his knees, arms upraised like the great titan condemned to bear the weight of the cosmos upon his shoulders in penance for his rebellion.

The *Lux Ferem* continued its descent, a falling sky of burning metal. Its dark shadow engulfed them all.

Thirty metres...

Magnus' mind buckled under the furious storm of aether raging within him. Gene-wrought flesh stretched drum-taut, every bone unseating from its neighbour as sinews stretched.

His synaptic connections overloaded to burnout.

Could anything fly so close to such power and live?

Magnus reached deep for everything he had left, but he had nothing more to give, no reserves to draw upon.

Then a solitary legionary limped from the firestorm, the gemstone upon his chest a too-bright beacon that spoke of their shared destiny.

+Ahriman,+ said Magnus. +Help us. Help *me!*+

The legionary broke the circle of the mandala, and stood before him. The Great Ocean swelled within him, stronger than any of his other sons. How had Magnus not seen this before?

Ahriman placed his hand upon the primarch's chest and threw his head back in agony as a measure of the power consuming his primarch passed into a body wholly unable to bear such a burden.

The power he passed to Magnus was fractional, a pebble in a field of boulders.

But even a pebble could start an avalanche.

Aether fire raged around them in a spinning conflagration, shrieking and blue like a murderous flock of azure raptors. Howling laughter surrounded them, a choir of voices that cackled with lunatic glee and wept with dour fatalism. Swirling discs of light spun like wind-blown petals, but the power they bore was fed into the combined magicks of Magnus and his Thousand Sons.

+It. Is. Working,+ Magnus cried out into the minds of his sons, feeling the inexorable descent of the mass-conveyor slowing.

And as the great alchymists of Old Earth knew...

+As above, so below!+

The power wrought and expended from the surface of Morningstar was incredible, a weaving of immaterial energies a mere handful of beings had ever dared to wield before.

And it was working.

Magnus stood at the centre of a circle of power, channelling incomprehensible energies to achieve the impossible. His flesh was pellucid and incandescent, an angelic form to equal anything born of Baal.

The mass of the *Lux Ferem* could not be stopped, but it could be slowed just enough. The city-sized weight of the mass-conveyor was barely ten metres overhead, Magnus and his warriors safe within the crater pushed up into its belly as the rest of the vessel settled on the platform with a groan of metal that went on and on until if felt like it would never stop.

But it did stop.

The *Lux Ferem* gently touched down on the platform it had only recently departed, kissing the ground with the tenderest touch. Its keel was broken and its mighty heart was spent. It would never fly again, and Morningstar would be its grave.

But the majority of those borne within its hull were still alive.

Magnus exhaled a breath of purest light and power, the last of the potent energies blazing from his fingertips and leaving him hollow and empty.

The light from his body slowly faded, leaving only embers and sparks from the cracked hull overhead as their illumination. For now they were cut off from the outside world, enclosed within the dome his force had pushed into the *Lux Ferem*'s hull.

'You did it, my lord,' whispered Ahriman, his features gaunt and drained like a consumptive.

Magnus nodded, too exhausted to speak. He did not trust his limbs to function nor his mind to form a coherent answer. He heard a rhythmic hammering sound, like a forge-master beating a blade into shape. It came over and over, like approaching thunder. Was he imagining it or was he simply hearing his heart finally giving out under the strain?

'You did it, my lord,' repeated Phosis T'kar.

'But at what cost?' replied Magnus, his gaze sweeping his immediate surroundings. His every breath was dry and metallic, his flesh searingly hot to the touch.

Twenty-four of his warriors lay dead around him, their bodies little more than empty suits of armour filled with the ashen remains of their flesh. Fine grey dust poured from their sundered plate and molten flex-joints. Only Ahriman and Phosis T'kar had survived the psychic storm.

'They are all dust,' said Magnus. 'Every one of them.'

A great and terrible guilt swept through Magnus as the hammering sounded again, louder this time, more insistent.

'What have I done?' he said as the last of his strength drained from his body and light flooded the cavern beneath the *Lux Ferem*. Magnus saw movement in the light, a vast being of burnished steel and fury, a titan in iron and yellow and black. He knew him, but could not name him.

He fell, but did not hit the ground.

'I have you, brother,' said Perturabo.

Evacuation crews debarked the refugees from the *Lux Ferem* as swiftly as possible, leading thousands of weeping civilians back to the camps beyond the city walls. Upon these walls were battle companies of Iron Warriors, who now patrolled as if the city were an embattled outpost. Trust was in short supply and all further launches from Morningstar were abandoned until a functioning air traffic control could be set up within the fortress of the Iron Warriors.

It had been the worst day in Morningstar's history. Not even the few short but violent wars that ravaged it in the centuries since its founding had claimed such a toll.

The earthquake in Attar had claimed over fifteen thousand lives, but the death toll would have been higher had it not been for the intervention of Legion forces. Magnus and his warriors had rescued over two thousand souls from the ruins, and the Stor-Bezashk corps of the Iron Warriors cleared roads, erected bridges over newly torn fissures and organised the flow of refugees from the destroyed city with an efficiency that had been sadly absent from the governor's staff.

Yet even amid such terrible suffering and loss of life, there were a few spots of light amid the darkness.

Mechanicum Cybernetica cohorts followed a transponder signal to recover Magos Tancorix, who marched unharmed from the shattered hills around Attar bearing the wounded body of Major Anton Orlov across his shoulders.

Konrad Vargha's unconscious body was borne from the wrecked Stormbird by Iron Warriors Apothecaries and taken to the medicae facilities within the Sharei Maveth.

Rescue crews found the hideously burned bodies of Vashti Eshkol and Magos Tessza Rom in the rubble of Calaena's orbital command centre. Incredibly, they had survived the blast, and were even now being treated with life-saving technologies.

Perturabo himself carried Magnus within his fortress.

His sons stationed in Calaena rallied to him, but he did not stir. Every one of them had been joined with him at the moment of his fall. They had all felt his pain and caught a momentary glimpse into the mind of a god.

Whether that knowledge would shape them for good or ill remained to be seen.

Category 10: ANNIHILATION
[Massive scale and duration – planetary event]

EIGHT

MISTAKES • A LEGENDARY NAME • MAKE THEM PAY

Magnus drifted on tides unknown.

An infinite white void surrounded him, without dimensions or points of reference. He did not know this place, but it was clearly not the Great Ocean.

Perhaps this was what it was like to die? Or was this what a mind experienced when it finally let slip the moorings of existence and gave in to death?

No, neither of those answers seemed satisfactory.

For all that he had no experience of dying, this did not feel like the end of his body of light.

He had no sensation of his flesh, no sight of the absurdly fragile silver thread that linked his power to his corporeal shell when soaring in the Great Ocean.

Perhaps he had reached too far, dared too greatly, and this was the price he must pay. His body lived, but it was no longer linked to his mind. He had seen aspirants fail in this way before and watched as their bodies wasted away without the spirit to sustain them.

Would that be his fate? Would his sons be forced to watch their sire fade, the skin pulling back on his skull, the flesh melting from

141

his bones? Or would his miraculous gene-forged body endure forever, leaving him trapped in this limbo state?

Who could know?

The great dramaturge had only scratched the surface of things when he called death 'the undiscovere'd country, from whose bourn no traveller returns'.

If this was his fate, then Magnus would have no regrets.

Better to have flown too close to the sun than never feel its heat...

'I am still alive,' he said, and his voice was thrown back at him as though he stood in the centre of a great amphitheatre.

Since no vistas were presenting themselves in this void, Magnus would conjure his own. If he was going to spend an eternity in this place, then he would be damned if he'd do it bored.

Memories surged around him, a series of snapshots from his life: the climb into the hills of Prospero where he found the statue whose destruction gave rise to the Fellowships of the Thousand Sons; the inaugural conclave of the First Masters in the Reflecting Cave; taking a knee before his father upon their first meeting in Occullum Square, though in truth they had spoken for many years already.

He conjured them at random, knowing all the while that nothing was every truly random, wondering which memory would come to the fore.

The answer presented itself, as the night he had climbed the Astartes Tower to meet his father on the eve of his departure from Terra swam into focus.

It had been a bittersweet moment, for they were both aware it would be many years before they met this way again. The Great Crusade was a vision of supreme ambition, one that would take father and sons to the uttermost corners of the galaxy for decades, perhaps even centuries. Only a fool would entertain any notions of certainty on the commencement of such a singular undertaking.

They had sat upon the highest peak of the slender tower and cast *their minds out over the world, flying together one last time. Only then did Magnus understand he was not simply witnessing a memory, but was part of it.*

Their bodies of light threaded the deep canyons of the Mid-Atalantic Ridge then circled the arid dust basin of the Mid-Terranean before following the Urals from Kara Oceanica to the Kievan Rus Khaganate. They circled Mount Narodnya, watching the ghosts of Fulgrim and Ferrus Manus as they competed over the labour of twin weapons.

'So perfect,' said the Emperor.

'Which one?' asked Magnus, but his father just smiled.

Magnus watched his brothers striving to outdo one another, finding their need to prove their superiority faintly ridiculous. What did it matter who could forge the best weapon when a primarch was a weapon unto himself?

'You are so like me in so many ways,' said the Emperor. *Magnus flushed with pride, but, as always, the Emperor's words carried multiple meanings.* 'You have a great many of my strengths, but strength magnified to excess eventually becomes a weakness.'

'How can that be?'

'Confidence can spill over into arrogance,' said the Emperor. 'An obsessive pursuit of perfection can blind you to what it costs to achieve. Attention to detail can become micro-management. Magnus, you have my intellect and my power, but like me you are prone to believing you can do no wrong, that your intellect lifts you above the risk of making petty mistakes or errors based on emotion.'

'What mistakes have I made?' asked Magnus, dreading the answer.

'Only time will tell what is a mistake and what is not, but an inability to believe you can ever make a mistake is dangerous. It leaves a mind open to certainty, and unwavering certainty is our greatest enemy. Always question and always be open to different ways of thinking, other ways of untangling the knot. That is the gift I give to you on this eve of our Crusade.'

'I do not understand.'

'You will, my son,' said the Emperor. 'Despite all I have just said, you are different enough from me that I can see how you will succeed where I have failed.'

'Failed? How have you failed?'

'I do not know yet,' said the Emperor with a wistful sheen to his subtle body. 'But I will soon, and I sense you and your favoured son must play a part in rectifying my mistakes.'

'My favoured son?' asked Magnus. 'They are all my sons.'

'There's truth in that, yes, but there is one who will bear your ambitions when you need them to travel farther than you could ever dream.'

'Where in this galaxy can I not travel?' said Magnus.

He felt his father's amusement.

'There are always places a son will travel where his father should not,' replied the Emperor. 'Just when you believe there is nothing more to be done, one of your sons will show you how wrong you have been all this time.'

'This sounds like gloomy advice, father,' said Magnus. 'I had hoped for something a little more inspiring as we venture out into the unknown.'

'What could be more inspiring than to know you have taught your sons to reach greater heights than you? They are your immortality, Magnus.'

No more had been said on the matter, and they had returned to their bodies atop the Astartes Tower to say farewell. His father had taken a seat by the great celestial occullum and the impossibly complex maps detailing His plans for galactic conquest. Though they had shared a sublime moment flying the aether, Magnus knew his time here was at an end. The Emperor turned and extended His hand, and Magnus looked into his father's eyes, wondering how he had not noticed the wistful look of sadness he now saw in them.

'Remember this moment,' said the Emperor.

'I will,' promised Magnus.

He took his father's hand and Magnus gasped in sudden pain as his spirit was wrenched from the memory and hurled back into his body.

Magnus opened his eye. Harsh lumen strips and hissing pipes hung from a ceiling of bare and brutal girders. The grim functionality of his surroundings sought to push the warm memory of his father from his mind.

Magnus knew better than to suppose his consciousness had fashioned that particular memory purely by chance.

What mistakes have I made on Morningstar?

Every atom in his body was bathed in fire.

Together with Ahriman and Phosis T'kar, Magnus marched through the arched, fresco-lined passageways of the Sharei Maveth. Iron Warriors flanked each intersection like knights of old and acid-etched blast doors lifted at every choke point. The interior of the Iron Warriors fortress was a beautiful death-trap, a series of cunning blind alleys, bottlenecks and crossfires that would make any assault suicidal.

Repercussive pain filled his bones with barbed wire, his veins with acid. He had known that such magnificent power could not be wielded without consequence, but this pain was beyond even his powers to ease.

'Perhaps you should have remained on the medicae level, my lord,' said Ahriman.

'I am grateful for your concern, Ahzek,' said Magnus, 'but I can tolerate this.'

'I do not pretend to know how deep your pain runs, my lord, but the Pavoni were fussing over you like a newborn.'

The image amused Magnus and he smiled, though even it sent a current of agony through the muscles of his face.

'How did I get here?'

'The Lord of Iron carried you,' said Phosis T'kar. 'He would not permit us to bear you.'

Magnus heard the strain in Phosis T'kar's voice, and felt his son's anger that someone – even a primarch – not of the XV Legion had borne his wounded lord.

'And how long have I been absent?'

'A day and a night,' answered Ahriman.

'What have I missed?'

'Morningstar is rushing to embrace its own extinction,' said Phosis T'kar. 'The last thirty hours have seen a sharp rise in attacks by the Sons of Shaitan – bombings, spree-killings and random acts of individual psychosis. We're seeing a wave of mass suicides in the refugee camps and escalating incidences of familial violence resulting in bloodshed.'

'The *Lux Ferem*?' asked Magnus.

'Fully evacuated,' said Ahriman. 'But there is something else you should know.'

'What?'

'Atharva and the warriors you sent to Zharrukin have not returned. We cannot raise them on the vox or contact them via psychic means.'

Magnus paused to consider Ahriman's news, taking a moment to allow a sudden nausea to pass. Clearly his sense of secrets buried in Zharrukin had been correct, but what danger had he sent his sons into?

'I will find them,' Magnus promised, letting out a hot breath. 'We do not leave any of our brothers behind.'

The pain wracking his mind and body was intense; his spine felt as if every vertebra was being inexorably crushed in a forge-vice, and his thoughts moved like glue through his mind.

He would be suffering this pain for weeks to come.

'Where does this increase in attacks put us in terms of getting the rest of Morningstar evacuated?'

He felt Ahriman and Phosis T'kar's reluctance to answer.

'Better the Lord of Iron tells you,' said Ahriman.

The heart of the Sharei Maveth had changed a great deal since Magnus had last seen it. Perturabo's sanctum still had the air of a workshop, but one with a series of impossible deadlines to meet. The vaulted space was now filled with new additions: hardwired cogitator banks drawing power from freshly installed battery racks, scores of lexmechanics and a hundred or more calculus logi passing linguascript at the speed of thought between adepts seconded from the Analyticae.

Magos Tancorix held court over the new arrivals, and directed his Mechanicum staff with vigour as they attempted to untangle the chaos that threatened to overwhelm the evacuation effort.

Perturabo and a dozen of his warriors watched from his elevated workshop, and Magnus winced as he climbed the steps to meet his brother.

Perturabo looked up as he approached, and his stoic expression lifted at the sight of Magnus. He stepped away from the warriors gathered around the table and shook his head.

'I have long held that it would take something immense to kill one of us,' said Perturabo, 'but I had no idea you would take that as a challenge.'

Magnus shrugged, masking the pain shooting down his spine.

'I had to do something,' said Magnus. 'I could not stand by and let so many die. You would have done the same.'

'Modesty doesn't suit you,' said Perturabo with a grin. 'I know I am strong, but even I would struggle to bear the weight of a starship.'

'It was not physical strength that saved the *Lux Ferem*.'

'I know, but it does not matter *how* you saved that ship, only that you did. Tales of your heroism will travel far from

Morningstar. The great primarch Magnus, who bore the weight of a vast starship upon his noble shoulders. This is how legends are born, brother.'

Magnus had not considered the idea of his act becoming widely known, but with troublesome rumours already circulating the crusading expeditionary fleets, perhaps a story to reinforce the positive aspects of the Thousand Sons' abilities would be no bad thing.

Perturabo nodded towards the viewscreen, calling up images of the many thousands of people beyond the city walls still awaiting rescue.

'Have your legionaries told you what the people of Morningstar are calling you now?' asked Perturabo. 'At least, the ones who aren't killing themselves in droves.'

'No, what?'

'They call you the Crimson King. It has a nice ring to it, don't you think?'

'That it does,' agreed Magnus.

Perturabo placed one hand on his shoulder, the other at his neck, pulling him close for a fraternal embrace.

His next words were for Magnus alone.

'You came a heartbeat from death,' he whispered. 'By all rights, you *should* have died. And our father's Great Crusade would have been robbed of one of its brightest sons, brighter even than dear Horus. More importantly, I would have lost a dear brother. There are none among our kin I regard as highly as you, so promise me you won't risk your life like that again.'

Magnus shrugged and said, 'We are warriors, Perturabo. Who among us can make such a promise?'

Perturabo released him and turned back to the screen.

'Heroic as it was, we are now faced with the burdensome task of recalculating the tally on who yet remains to be evacuated from Morningstar.'

'Are you saying I shouldn't have saved the *Lux Ferem*?'

'Not at all – we came here to save lives.'

'Then I do not understand.'

Perturabo called up a view of Calaena's port facilities. The *Lux Ferem* lay shattered across the landing platforms, its keel split and gaping wounds in the hull exposing the vessel's iron guts. Mechanicum breaker units under the direction of the wounded Tessza Rom swarmed the ship, cutting it apart like oceanic hunters harvesting a slaughtered leviathan.

'You saved the ship, but its wreckage now blocks fully a third of Calaena's platforms,' said Perturabo. 'Mistress Eshkol informs me it will take at least four days to render them usable again, and even with the newly constructed landing facilities beyond the city walls, my best estimate predicts only a third of those who boarded the mass-conveyor will escape.'

Magnus was appalled. 'So even though I saved the *Lux Ferem*, most of the people it carried will still die?'

'Regrettably so. We have not the ship assets nor, as it turns out, the time to save them.'

'But we had months before Morningstar became unstable.'

'We did. Now we do not.'

'Were your calculations in error?'

A flash of irritation crossed Perturabo's face. 'They were not. Something fundamental has changed.'

'How is that possible?'

'I do not know. See for yourself.'

The primarch of the Iron Warriors swept away the image of the *Lux Ferem*'s hulk and replaced it with a wavering hololithic image of Morningstar. Innumerable cyclone-like storms swirled over the sphere's volume, growing and multiplying with terrifying speed and ferocity. Their motion was unpredictable, each changing direction at random, joining with others or breaking apart into hyper-violent local tempests.

'These are Morningstar's geomagnetic field patterns,' said Perturabo, rotating the globe with deft swipes of his palm.

Magnus studied the patterns shifting over the globe. The motion of the undulating storm fronts and magnetic dissonance put him in mind of a deep and turbulent ocean. The normal flow of energy around the planet was hideously disrupted, and patterns that ought to be regular and unidirectional were jagged and inconstant.

And yet...

Magnus stepped closer to the command table, shifting the lambent globe and drinking in the information. He let the ebb and flow of the magna-storms wash over him.

'I see something,' he said, trying not to let the elusive thought slip away. 'Something in the depths of the flow, something *unnatural.*'

Magnus shifted his mind into the fourth Enumeration, the realm of abstraction, coaxing revelation instead of forcing it into the light. Something in the evolution of the growth patterns shared by the storms felt awry, as though it were governed by an equation so complex, so fractal, it was all but invisible.

'This is not random,' he said, now seeing the beauty underpinning it all. 'The patterns move like music or deep ocean currents, but they are *not* the result of natural interactions. The source of these storms is man-made.'

'Man-made?' said Perturabo. 'Someone did this deliberately?'

Magnus nodded, seeing more of the pattern emerge as the grammar of the storms coalesced in his mind.

'If Magos Tancorix can develop an inverse algorithm capable of breaking down the mathematics of these flows...'

'We can find the source,' finished Perturabo.

Wind-driven rain fell in torrential sheets over the platforms atop the Sharei Maveth, lashing the hulls of the two Stormbirds, one gunmetal grey, the other vivid crimson. Lingering propellant fumes choking the upper atmosphere made the rain pitch black and mildly acidic. Portions of the gunships' hulls were streaked where the paint was thinnest.

'It looks like Morningstar is stripping them of their identity,' said Ahriman.

'But no such damage is accruing to your war-plate, brother,' said Phosis T'kar, cupping his hands and letting them fill with dark rain that looked like oil.

Ahriman looked down at his armour and saw that Phosis T'kar was right. Even in the gloom of the oncoming storm and the flickering lightning, the hue of his plate was still vividly crimson.

'I will try to take that as a positive sign,' he said, trying not read anything into this peculiarity.

'You should,' advised Phosis T'kar. 'You have become too glum of late, Ahzek. We are almost done with this place, and soon we will be back on the Crusade, doing the Emperor's work!'

Phosis T'kar stood and let the rain fall from his palms. He rubbed his gauntlets together as if washing his hands. Ahriman turned his head to the sky and the coruscating atmosphere.

A planet-wide lightning storm was brewing, the sky blazing in all directions as if a distant conflagration were slowly closing on the city like a noose. Ahriman knew that wasn't literally true, but as a metaphor it was perfectly apt.

'This is how a planet ought to meet its end,' said Phosis T'kar. 'Fighting to the last and raging at its extinction.'

'I have had my fill of worlds ending,' said Ahriman. 'We embarked on this endeavour to save the Emperor's realm, not to watch it die.'

'Not every world can be saved,' said Phosis T'kar. 'Maybe not every world *deserves* to be saved.'

Ahriman rounded on Phosis T'kar. 'What do you mean by that?'

The Raptora adept shrugged. 'This planet's roots are weak. The Imperium should not be built on worlds whose foundations are crumbling.'

'And who would make that decision?' asked Ahriman. 'You?'

'Why not? Are we not the foremost Legion in intellect? Do we not divine the future? If we cannot know better than any other which worlds will provide good footings for the Emperor's dominion, then who else can? Would you trust *them*?'

Phosis T'kar nodded in the direction of the Iron Warriors, giants with reflected bolts of lightning glittering upon their armour. Before Ahriman could answer, his mouth filled with the taste of blood and ash, of melting glass and steel. The recurring image of rain falling in endless sheets sent a jolt of horror through him, a sense of foreboding so strong it all but overwhelmed him.

Perturabo conferred with his Techmarines as his warriors boarded their Stormbird, and Ahriman's gaze was drawn inexorably to Forrix, a warrior who had been as good as dead and ready for interment in a Dreadnought sarcophagus until Ahriman's unchecked power had healed him. The only sign of the warrior's near death was a slight limp, but Ahriman saw a dark halo wreathing him, an effect that ancient shamans had known and feared as a death mark.

Could any of his brothers see it? Or was this merely an echo of the vision he had seen of the monstrous destiny ahead of Forrix?

He turned away, the sight of the Iron Warrior stirring a bone-deep nausea within him.

'Is something wrong?' asked Phosis T'kar.

'What?'

'Your weapon.'

Ahriman looked down and saw he had his hand on the grip of his bolter. He eased his finger carefully from the trigger.

'Apologies, brother,' he said, wishing to make light of the lapse in weapon discipline. 'Ever since the attack on the *Lux Ferem*, my seersight has me jumping at shadows.'

'Good. That's your survival instinct kicking in,' replied Phosis T'kar. 'One of those shadows might be dangerous.'

Ahriman nodded, already well aware that Forrix was something supremely dangerous, even if he could not yet understand how.

He let out a breath and forced himself to look away.

XV Legion Techmarines tended the hull of Magnus' gunship, prepping it for a flight into hostile atmospherics. They fitted deflection conductors, ceramite insulators and ablative plates over sensitive components that could be burned out by a rogue electromagnetic burst.

'We're ready,' said Phosis T'kar, standing taller and pushing out his chest as Magnus emerged from the belly of the Stormbird. The primarch conferred briefly with his Techmarines, then nodded and waved them aboard.

The Thousand Sons marched onto the gunship, twenty-five in all, and swiftly took their assigned seats along its up-armoured fuselage. Ahriman and Phosis T'kar were the last to board and were standing on the embarkation ramp when Perturabo came over to speak to his brother.

'Good hunting, Magnus,' said the Lord of Iron. 'May you find your missing sons alive and unharmed.'

Magnus nodded and said, 'And may you find the source of Morningstar's pain, brother.'

'I will,' said Perturabo. His gravel-voiced certainty left Ahriman in no doubt he would. 'And then I will destroy it.'

'Even if you do, there is no saving this world.'

'I know,' said Perturabo, offering his brother his hand. 'It will be an act of vengeance, nothing more, but that will be enough for me.'

'It will need to be enough for all of us,' said Magnus, taking Perturabo's hand.

As the Lord of Iron returned to his gunship, Ahriman saw a look of profound sadness in his primarch's face.

'My lord?' he said, and the moment passed. 'Is something wrong?'

'Nothing,' said Magnus, turning and striding down the troop compartment to take his place at the head of his warriors.

What had Magnus seen when he gripped his brother's hand?

Did he see every secret thought hidden? Would such knowledge be a blessing or a curse?

Looking over at the Iron Warriors Stormbird, Ahriman knew exactly which it was.

Vashti watched the Stormbirds lift off in a haze of jetwash and vaporised rain through the toughened glass of the makeshift control centre. Mechanicum adepts had built it on a cleared gun platform on the highest tower of the Sharei Maveth and hurriedly wired it into the operating systems of the fortress.

Barely functional was the expression that leapt to Vashti's mind when she first saw her new working environment.

Together with Tessza Rom and a staff of calculus logi, she had resumed her duties coordinating airspace around Calaena after only ten hours in the medicae levels to treat her grievous wounds.

An atomiser misted aerosolised water and counterseptic over her burned face. She tried to blink then remembered she couldn't. The fire in the command centre had vaporised the protective layers from her eyes, and until grafts and augmetics could be sourced, she relied on the atomisers.

Her arms and back had been scorched black, but dropping

behind her command console had saved her life from Korinna Moreno's treacherous blast. A constant flow of stimms kept the worst of the pain at bay, but even so, she hurt in a dozen places and her every movement was cripplingly slow.

Still, she had been inordinately lucky: only she and Tessza Rom had made it out alive.

If what Tessza had become could be called living.

The scraps of her friend's ruined body hung suspended, foetus-like, in an amniotic tank in the centre of the makeshift control centre. Cognitive enhancers hung like pulsing snakes from the rear of her cranium, boosting her ability to sift the cascades of data surrounding her in twitching fog banks of noospheric light.

Princeps of the Collegia Titanicus sometimes commanded their giant war-engines in a similar manner, and it was said the connection to the Omnissiah was sublime. Vashti could understand that, but the thought of her life spent as a wraith preserved in bio-suspension gel made her skin crawl. Tessza's body was broken beyond repair, but her mind was more agile than ever.

'Gunships will be safe-distance clear in six seconds,' said Tessza, her voice grating from the brass vox-horn hung from wires in the corner of the bare plascrete chamber. 'Operational timetable resuming in ten seconds.'

'Handoffs logged and ready,' replied Vashti. 'I have fifty-four ships making stacked figure of eights overhead. Let's use the extra time they've given us.'

Vashti had suspended flight operations for seven minutes to allow the Legions a window to get their ships prepped and beyond Calaena's airspace. As it turned out, they'd only needed half that time.

With the downing of the *Lux Ferem* and the loss of the platforms for at least another two days, what trans-orbital ships they had were being pressed into making faster and more frequent trips between the fleet and the surface.

Pushing ships and crews so hard was beyond dangerous, but what other choice was there?

Vashti studied the crackling, static-washed panels before her. Calaena was all but abandoned, the people who'd thronged the city's streets now camped at the foot of the Sharei Maveth's walls. For a time, the sky over the fortress had remained clear and still, even as Calaena burned and localised magna-tempests sent lightning ripping along its streets.

Tens of thousands had pressed against the distant edges of the fortress' outworks, seeking safety in the lee of its towering walls. The Iron Warriors had been forced to deactivate the minefields and open the gates on the outer walls to allow Morningstar's people to approach.

Now an ocean of humanity pressed up against the fortress, stretching all the way back to the edges of the city. At least a hundred thousand or more, though with census information woefully out of date, it was impossible to know for certain.

'Focus, Mistress Eshkol,' replied Tessza, all traces of the humanity she had once possessed in abundance now absent from her voice. Her friend's body endured, but what had made her human was all but gone.

Vashti nodded and turned her attention from the thousands of people at the foot of the walls to the orbital tracks and streams of data being updated every second.

In her last free second before Vashti took on the burden of getting as many people as she could off-world, she glanced down at the tracks of the two gunships as they slowly diverged. One raced north towards Zharrukin, the other due west towards the centre of Morningstar's last remaining ocean.

'Find what you're looking for,' said Vashti, angrier than she could ever remember. 'Make the bastards pay for what they've done here.'

NINE

SURVIVOR • TO THE GRAVE • WHAT DID THEY DO?

Planet-wide hurricanes were engulfing the rest of Morningstar, but Zharrukin was now a peaceful eye in the global storm. The city had been all but obliterated, yet enough architectural clues remained for Magnus to picture it as he had last seen it.

'This region should be suffering shear-force magna-storms and violent tectonic upheaval,' said Ahriman, staring up into the clear, cloudless sky. 'How is this possible?'

No one had an answer. Not even Magnus.

Studying Morningstar's magnetic polarity readings on the journey from Calaena had provided no clue as to why this one area among all others should escape the violence. That Calaena too was suffering far less than the rest of the planet spoke of design and intent, but to what end?

The primarch's new Stormbird sat cooling a hundred metres from another gunship in the colours of the Thousand Sons. Its hull was windblown, its engines cold. Dust swirled around the opened assault ramp.

'Looks abandoned,' said Phosis T'kar, chopping his hand left. Two squads of legionaries moved to flank the gunship. Ahriman gestured right and his squads mirrored those of Phosis T'kar.

'It isn't,' said Magnus, striding directly towards the gunship. 'Someone is still alive on board. A mortal.'

They approached the gunship cautiously, every legionary's bolter trained unerringly on the entrance to the crew compartment. Magnus touched the mind within, feeling her fear and uncertainty. He knew her immediately and held up his fist.

'Stand down,' he said. 'Ahriman, Phosis T'kar, with me.'

Magnus boarded the gunship and swiftly made his way along the troop compartment towards the cockpit. The door hung open, its locking mechanism blasted open by a mass-reactive round. The weapon that had fired it sat propped up by the open door.

Magnus ducked into the cockpit and saw Niko Ashkali slumped in the co-pilot's chair, her skin pallid and her lips cracked and dry.

'How long has she been here?' said Ahriman.

'Long enough to risk trying Legion-issue supplies,' said Magnus, bending to lift two foil wrappers and a dripping hydration pack discarded at her feet.

'Throne! Is she still alive?'

'Barely,' said Magnus, reaching into the conservator's physiology with his power. Her pulse was weak and thready, fluttering like a wounded bird. Hostile interactions from the Legion rations she had ingested ravaged her system.

'Did she not know our food and drink are poisonous to humans?' asked Phosis T'kar.

'Maybe she did, but decided it was worth the risk to try and stay alive a little longer,' said Magnus, easing into the seventh Enumeration and driving the chemicals inimical to mortal physiology from her system.

The effect was almost instantaneous.

Niko Ashkali bent double and vomited over the console of the Stormbird, retching hard as her damaged system purged itself of toxins. Magnus kept the connection between them open, using his power to renew her struggling cells and undo the terrible damage that the chemical-heavy nutrients had wreaked.

She took a huge gasp of air and her eyes stretched wide.

'Easy, Mistress Ashkali, easy,' said Magnus. 'You are safe now. You are safe.'

'What...' she said, her eyes struggling to focus on Magnus' face. 'I... What happened?'

'You partook of Legion combat rations,' said Magnus. 'Such fare is engineered to enhance a Space Marine's biology and boost his effectiveness in combat. It is all but lethal to mortals. You are lucky your heart did not give out under the strain.'

Ashkali managed a weak smile, wiping the sleeve of her robes across her mouth and spitting an acrid wad to the deck plates.

'Sorry,' she said, looking over at the dripping mess on the avionics panel. 'I think I ruined your gunship.'

'Do not fret,' said Magnus. 'We have others.'

Ashkali twisted in the seat, looking past Magnus to Ahriman and Phosis T'kar.

'Is Atharva with you? Has he come out yet?'

'No, we have had no contact with Atharva since he left Calaena,' said Magnus. 'We are here to find him. Do you know where he is?'

Ashkali nodded. 'Yes, he and the others went down into the ship.'

'What ship?'

'The colony ship, the one the storm exposed.'

'Show me,' said Magnus.

Something tore farther back along the Stormbird's hull. Perturabo heard it clatter down the length of the fuselage. He flicked his eyes down onto the control panel, looking for fresh warning signs.

The panel was already rich with warning indicators, so it was hard to tell what damage was new. He'd deactivated a great many of them, the sounds blurring together as if the gunship itself were screaming in pain.

The view through the streaked armourglass canopy was the very vision of the apocalypse. Sky and ocean were impossible to tell apart. Both were all but obscured by the ferocious storms raging all the way to the Kármán line. Forks of lightning split the sky in stroboscopic flashes and booming peals of thunder swatted the gunship as though it were an insect in a hurricane.

The first storm hit five kilometres from Calaena, a spiteful cyclonic tempest that came out of nowhere and almost dragged them to the raging swells of dark water before Perturabo fought them back into the sky. Another all but shorted out their guidance system until Obax Zakayo was able to jerry-rig a makeshift insulation cowl. Ferocious lightning battered the hull, the gunship's wings trailing purple-and-blue streamers of electric fire from newly welded conductor rods.

The Stormbird juddered under Morningstar's assaults: hurricane-force winds, typhoon rains and pulsing electromagnetic squalls that made for heart-pounding moments of uncertainty when the engines threatened to cut out.

The Iron Warriors gunship threaded the needle of the worst storms, surviving thanks to a mixture of near real-time data from Magos Tancorix and Perturabo's phenomenal skill as a pilot.

Barban Falk stood behind him in the hatchway to the troop compartment, where the rest of the Iron Warriors sat in stoic silence. Falk held the bulkhead in a white-knuckled grip.

'My lord,' he began, 'the ship is tearing itself apart!'

'I know, Barban,' said Perturabo, wrestling the controls as torsion forces tried to twist the gunship's keel apart. He spun the gunship, feathering the engines and pushing the prow up to ride the spiralling forces. Metal screamed as he pushed the Stormbird far beyond the limits of its performance envelope. Something else tore loose, and another warning light blinked angrily in front of him.

'My lord,' said Falk, pushing forwards and hurriedly strapping himself into the co-pilot's seat, 'how can you even navigate this?'

Perturabo grunted and glanced up through the canopy, seeing the swirling madness of the star-maelstrom even through the terrifying power of Morningstar's global tempest.

'This isn't the worst storm I know,' said Perturabo.

'It's not?'

'No, and we are not turning back. Not now. The source is just ahead.'

'That's not what I was going to suggest, my lord.'

'Then what were you going to say?'

'Very well, yes, it *was* what I was going to suggest,' said Falk, looking deep into the onrushing storms as flickers of pulsing lightning lit up the gunship's interior. 'I just want to know what purpose you think this mission serves.'

Perturabo didn't answer at first.

'I want to destroy whatever is killing this world,' he muttered eventually.

'Magos Tancorix said it was already too late to reverse what is happening to Morningstar,' said Falk. 'Finding and destroying the source of these storms will not change that.'

'I know,' said Perturabo, hauling the controls to pull away from a rapidly developing electromagnetic tornado. The gunship howled in protest, but its pain eased as he levelled out again.

'Then why are we out here, my lord?' asked Falk. 'Why are we risking our lives to do this?'

'Because I will not leave Morningstar without hitting back at our enemies,' snapped Perturabo. 'I will not allow this world to die without exacting a blood price for its ending.'

Falk nodded. 'Well, why didn't you just say so?'

'Because it is a reaction that springs from emotion, and I have a reputation to maintain.'

Falk gripped his seat tighter as the gunship made a gut-loosening lurch downwards. Kilometre-high tsunamis threatened to smash them from the sky.

'Your secret is safe with me,' he said. 'I think I'll be taking it to my grave.'

Perturabo chuckled and pushed the gunship into a shallow dive as the wavering display on the panels indicated they had reached the source of Morningstar's apocalypse.

He guided the gunship towards a looming, cliff-like wall of darkness, beyond which nothing could be seen, and within which only electromagnetic chaos awaited.

'Hold on,' he said. 'We're going in.'

The hatch had been designed for beings of mortal stature, but Magnus ducked down and climbed inside the body of the colony ship. Beyond was a cramped airlock with brushed steel walls inset with ceramic tiles. The floor was canted slightly to the side, telling him the ship had not come down straight.

The door at the far end of the chamber was wide open, and Magnus saw a long corridor of similar design, its ceiling hung with crackling cables that spat pale sparks to provide fitful illumination.

He moved through the airlock and into the corridor, each squad following the line of the walls with their bolters locked hard to their shoulders. Magnus pushed his mind into the lower Enumerations and stretched his senses out before him. He felt no threat and no life from within, but he kept his martial abilities close to the surface. Bitter experience during his years of conquest had taught Magnus that not everything seeking to inflict harm could be detected by psychic means.

Some unseen mechanism detected their presence, and the few remaining glow-globes strung from the ceiling girders flickered to life. Stuttering illumination flowed down the corridor, revealing featureless walls with cracked windows and sealed shutter-doors to either side. Rust-coloured stains were smeared on the lower reaches of the wall, and it was impossible to interpret them as anything other than bloodied handprints.

'Of course there would be blood,' said Ahriman, taking position at Magnus' left shoulder.

'Now all we need are bodies,' added Phosis T'kar.

Magnus moved along the corridor towards a circular intersection. He glanced through each window as he passed, but the glass was opaque with age and thick with smoke damage. He could see nothing within, and the stale smell of emptiness hung in the air.

He checked each door as he passed.

'Anything?' asked Phosis T'kar on his right, flickering kine energies playing across his fingertips.

'Sealed fast, just like the hatch,' said Magnus, reaching an intersection that split the corridor into four identical passageways. Red-and-gold lettering offered clues to what lay at the end of each.

'Can you read this?' asked Ahriman.

'Given time,' said Magnus. 'It is the language of the fallen Dragon Nations.'

'Atharva was always obsessed by those lands,' said Phosis T'kar.

'Perhaps his fondness for the eastern empires drew him onwards when he ought to have been more cautious,' said Ahriman.

Magnus nodded towards the faded symbol of a winged, serpent-entwined staff on the bulkheads above each corridor.

'This was a medicae deck,' he said.

More flaking blood stained the walls here, arterial by the volume and width of its arc. Magnus paused and placed a palm flat on the walls, feeling a soft but regular pulse of vibration in the steelwork. A lingering sense of dread permeated his senses, a memory of terrible pain, though he could not locate any source for the feeling.

'This way,' said Magnus, crossing the intersection and following the line of glow-globes.

The advancing Thousand Sons found every corridor more or less identical, stripped of identifying markings and redolent of the ancient age of spacefaring. No trace remained of any crew or records, though they found many more bloodstains. None of the data terminals they passed had power, but they had not the means to access them even if they had. The only sounds were their echoing footfalls and the crackle of vox static in their helmets.

Magnus' every breath was freighted with a growing sense of the endless pain sealed within. This had been a medicae ship, so such a feeling should not have been unexpected, but he sensed more than just the *memory* of pain.

He sensed *enduring* pain.

They followed the trail of glow-globes and ruptured cable-lines, passing derelict rooms filled with empty gurneys, banks of haphazardly stacked machines and stowage bays where ungainly suits of hermetically sealed exo-armour lay in disarray. The deeper into the ship they went, the more it reeked of abandonment, and the more wary Magnus became.

'So many relics,' he said.

'It's junk,' said Phosis T'kar.

'It is *history*,' said Ahriman.

'Then why has none of it been removed?'

No answer readily presented itself. The interior of this ship was a treasure trove of incredible artefacts from a distant age, a time capsule that could offer invaluable insight to the Golden Age of Man.

And yet it had been left hidden beneath the ground.

The trail of glow-globes eventually led to an echoing vaulted chamber filled with towering banks of machinery and glass-fronted coffin-capsules. Each was filled with a stagnant mire, rancid and opaque, fed by coiled hoses that dripped viscous fluids to the deck. Thousands of these cryo-tubes lined the walls, arranged in rows that vanished into the darkness of the chamber. A number were punctured with what looked like gunshots, but many others were still functional, their surfaces limned with frost and venting wisps of condensing air.

The Thousand Sons spread out as Magnus advanced, forming an arrowhead with their primarch at the tip of the barb.

Beneath each gleaming cylinder was a metallic gurney bolted to the floor and fitted with leather straps and a needle-filled cranial restraint. Where the rest of the ship felt abandoned, little more than structure to house the ship's true purpose, this chamber still had function and intent.

Magnus hated it.

His every sense was screaming, telling him to escape while he could. He tensed as his body instinctively readied itself for fight or flight. An animal reaction, one he had thought himself above, but evidently not.

'What is it?' said Ahriman, reading the change in his aura. 'Where is the threat?'

'There is none,' said Magnus, though the words felt like an ashen lie. 'None I can see, at least.'

'What were they doing here?' asked Phosis T'kar, lowering his bolter and standing before one of the gurneys. He knelt and dragged out a footlocker pushed beneath it. He flipped open the lid, finding it filled with rings, necklaces and all manner of jewellery that gleamed like a miser's hoard.

'What is this?' he said, scooping a handful of rings and bracelets and holding it out to Magnus. 'They brought all this from Old Earth?'

A swirling, unfocused nausea swept over Magnus for no easily identifiable reason. He felt sick to his stomach at the idea of touching the jewellery.

'Put it back,' he said. 'Now.'

'Why?'

'Just do it!'

Phosis T'kar shrugged and tossed the items back onto the pile. He rose to his feet as a suffocating fear arose in Magnus, a sensation he had not felt since...

...since he had watched his sons being torn apart by a sickness erupting from within their own flesh...

The image was so distorted and half-formed it felt like it belonged to someone else, a sick recreation of a half-heard rumour, a conjured fiction of suppressed horror.

'What did they do here?' he said. 'Throne of Terra, what did they do...?'

A yammering host of hideously conjoined voices, simmering with potent and enduring rage, answered from the darkness.

Tore us from ourselves...

Cut the silver cord...

Denied us our potential...

Magnus spun to look down the length of the chamber, seeing a coalescing bleed of ferocious psychic energy. The pain and the horror inflicted here did not rest easy. Nor was it forgiving.

Six figures stood in the midst of this bleed.

Legionary bulk, silhouetted in a sick, rippling undersea glow. Magnus knew these warriors; they were his sons, but... *changed*.

'We have to leave here,' said Ahriman. 'Right now.'

'No,' said Magnus. 'Not yet.'

'...too late to leave,' said one of the figures, stepping from the light.

Sick dread settled in Magnus' stomach as the figure's identity became clear.

'Much too late,' Atharva repeated. 'No one leaves Shai-Tan.'

The darkness was unyielding and absolute.

Perturabo's spatial awareness was instantly overturned as the gunship flipped around. The very forces of creation hurled them into the teeth of the storm, and the Stormbird's hull screeched as chaotic forces sought to crush it. The control column was torn from his grip.

'This madness is going to rip us apart!' cried Falk.

Perturbo shook his head and took the control column in both hands. 'Not while I have my strength it won't.'

The column juddered like a wild beast, resisting him as he fought to level them out. Gravitic and electromagnetic forces wrenched the Stormbird in every direction. The gunship's instruments were useless, the gyroscope or avionics panel flashing with meaningless and contradictory information. They were climbing, diving, spinning, yawing and rolling all at the same time.

Finding what was level was next to impossible.

But Perturabo had a North Star better than any instrumentation. He couldn't see the star-maelstrom that always watched him from afar, but he could sense it. He felt its presence like a solid anchor, a fixed point of reference that he was, for once, glad to have at his back.

Perturabo pushed out the engines, the muscles of his arms bunching and swelling as he held the gunship true to its course. The forces acting on it were titanic and elemental, but he was the Lord of Iron and there was no give in him.

As if sensing he would not yield, the tempest's force dropped away, and the gunship shot into the eye of the storm like a bullet from a gun.

The sudden stillness was shocking after such roiling chaos, and the Stormbird shuddered in release. Perturabo pushed it into a slow, downward curve.

'Mother of Olympia...' said Barban Falk. 'What is that?'

Perturabo had no answer.

The ocean was boiling as far as the eye could see, its surface churned white by plumes of superheated vapour geysering from its surface. Directly below them was a sprawling agglomeration of force-shielded steel with foundations plunging deep into the water. In scale it matched the orbital shipyards of Jupiter, a machined metropolis afloat on the ocean.

'Did Morningstar ever have an orbital plate like Vaalbara or Rodina?' asked Falk, still trying to process the scale of what had been built here. 'Perhaps it crashed? Is that what I'm looking at?'

'This is not the remains of a crashed orbital plate,' said Perturabo. 'This was *built*.'

The gunship circled a series of wave-lashed towers, vast as hive blocks, their flanks pulsing with colossal energies.

Within the circumference of the towers, an area surely hundreds of kilometres in diameter, the ocean poured into a depthless crevasse that made the plunging mountain canyons of Olympia look like tiny cracks.

Perturabo angled the gunship down, drawing their flight towards the thunderous cascade of water. Pulling around, he saw the titanic walls of the crevasse were banded with layers that spoke of the geological ages of the world.

'That rock hasn't shown its face to the sun in millions of years,' said Falk.

Perturabo knew what this was, but couldn't believe it.

He pointed to the splits in the sedimentary layers and the clean breaks between the various aeons of rock.

'This is the edge of a tectonic plate,' he said as he began to understand the extraordinary feat of engineering that had been wrought here.

Perturabo had spent years exploring the mountains of Olympia to learn the strength of stone. He understood the deep time of geology and the millions of years it took to make or unmake a world. Yet this was happening right before his eyes.

'This city-machine is pushing one tectonic plate beneath another,' said Perturabo, his mind of metal and stone working to process the enormity and impossibility of what was happening to Morningstar. 'The Magos Geologicus have long hypothesised that a continental plate of sufficient magnitude being pushed under another and into the mantle could, over time, disrupt a planet's geomagnetic field. But the rate of subduction is usually only a few centimetres a year, and the effects would be so gradual as to be all but invisible in a mortal lifetime.'

'Well this is certainly visible,' replied Falk.

The towering cliffs within the crevasse plunged hundreds of kilometres into the planet's depths. Avalanches of rock fell into its hellish maw, the farthest depths of which were like ancient representations of the dread underworld where damned souls suffered torment for eternity.

'They built this with one purpose, and one purpose only,' said Perturabo in disbelief. 'To destroy their world.'

'The resources and technological expertise this would have required are immense,' said Falk. 'How could those Sons of Shaitan fanatics build such a thing, let alone keep its construction secret from Imperial command?'

Perturabo had been pondering the same thing, and the answer was so glaringly obvious he was angry he hadn't come to it earlier.

'They didn't need to,' he said.

'What do you mean?'

'Because they are one and the same,' said Perturabo.

'Who are you?' demanded Magnus.

'Surely you recognise your own flesh and blood?' said the thing within Atharva's body. The legionary's outline was haloed with light, as if myriad stab-lights were trained upon him, each casting a fuliginous shadow over the other.

'You speak through my son, but you are *not* him,' said Magnus. 'Dispense with this vile charade. What is your name?'

'My name is legion, for we are many, but you shall know us as Shai-Tan.'

'Shai-Tan? That name has meaning to this world.'

Atharva's body raised its arms like a preacher in a fane, and unchecked psychic energy bled from the fingertips like droplets of mercury. Sourceless winds blew and the dust of millennia spun in maddened vortices on the floor.

'It is the name of this vessel,' said Shai-Tan, running his fingers over the walls and leaving painfully bright trails carved in the metal. 'A seed ship from a long-dead empire of Old Earth, it crossed the endless gulf of space with tens of thousands of hopeful souls in search of a better tomorrow.'

The voice was Atharva's, but with many more interleaved, ten thousand tormented souls finally able to voice their fury.

'What happened to you?' asked Magnus.

'*We died!*' yelled Shai-Tan, and a storm of kine force surged down the chamber like the blast wave of an orbital barrage.

Magnus leaned into Shai-Tan's power. His warriors were hurled back, slammed into bulkheads and falling in disarray. They were on their feet seconds later, bolter slides racked back, ready to open fire.

'My lord,' said Ahriman, 'do we shoot?'

'No,' said Magnus. 'These are your brothers.'

'Once. Now they are our vessels,' said Shai-Tan.

Shai-Tan and the other Space Marines advanced from the sick shimmer of psionic light. Their movements were stiff and awkward, as if the animating force within them was still reacquainting itself with the mechanics of flesh.

'Tell me what happened here,' said Magnus with a slow and measured tone.

'You already know, or at least you suspect,' said Shai-Tan, weaving spitting balls of lighting upon his fingertips as fire built in his eyes.

'Tell me.'

'No. I want *you* to say it,' said Shai-Tan, casting the ball lightning from his hand. Magnus met it with power of his own, grunting as flaring heat seared him. The fire died between them, and Magnus quashed his warriors' renewed aggression with Athanaean subtlety.

He took a step towards Shai-Tan, stretching into the farthest reaches of the Enumerations. He drank in the blistering aura of the psychic essence, feeling thousands of burning souls howling their pain within his son's captive flesh. Their fury was deep and brittle as fractured glass, volatile as raw fyceline.

Magnus exhaled, his breath misting before him as the temperature dropped sharply. He felt the sudden build up of aetheric power. Crushing force threw him into the chamber's walls and pinned him like a specimen awaiting study.

Reeking chemical preservatives from the shattered cryo-tube soaked him. A corpse sagged over his shoulder, bloated and bleach-pale, the flesh hanging in loose, sodden folds.

No raptures could keep the Thousand Sons from retaliating at this attack on their primarch. Disciplined volleys of mass-reactive rounds blazed. A blizzard of psychic fire surged in response and the bolter shells exploded in mid-air.

'A planet's worth of stolen psychic potential, and you fight it with guns?' said Shai-Tan.

'Stop this!' shouted Magnus, but violence was inevitable.

The power within Atharva's body unleashed a devastating psychic scream and three of Magnus' warriors were instantly immolated, flesh burning like magnesium flares within their armour. Two were ripped asunder by hyper-violent kine force, like traitors of antiquity pulled apart by horses. Another four turned their weapons upon themselves, firing explosive shells through their own helmets.

Psionic force shrieked up and down the chamber as Magnus' warriors cast off the shackles of restraint. Their powers were honed by a primarch's teachings and Prosperine discipline.

They were the mightiest psychic warriors in the galaxy.

And still, Shai-Tan's power was stronger.

Its was a fury that had grown beneath the world for millennia. Fire, lightning and raw force raged as the Thousand Sons fought their brothers taken by Shai-Tan.

Chemicals once benign, but now curdled to hideous toxicity, burned in rivers as cryo-tubes exploded in the crossfire and spilled yet more noxiously bloated corpses to the deck. Mass-reactive rounds and bolts of aether fire ricocheted from the walls. Metal buckled and twisted in outpourings of kine energy.

Shai-Tan stood before Magnus and lifted the head of the corpse behind him by its lank and rotted hair. Flesh sloughed from the softened skull like melted rubber. A stinking gruel of dissolved brain matter poured out through its eye sockets.

'Do you know what these machines did?' asked Shai-Tan.

Magnus spat a stinking brew of dead fluids and chemicals. 'No.'

'Liar!' roared Shai-Tan with deafening force.

What glass remained in the tubes blew out like explosions of splintered diamonds. Shards fell like daggers, and Magnus felt a momentary twist in his gut at the sight of broken and spinning glass.

Bodies slumped from every tube, every one of them pallid and distended with preservatives after millennia of immersion. The floor swam with stinking liquid, viscous and repulsive.

Magnus' seersight caught fleeting glimpses of endless rows of men, women and children strapped to the metal gurneys. He heard their screams rip through his skull. The sound was raw and animal, a sound no mortal throat should make, as the psychic potential of their minds was ripped out.

'Throne, no...' he said.

'You see now, yes?' said Shai-Tan.

'Yes,' sobbed Magnus.

Their suffering was beyond anything Magnus had thought possible. That people had *chosen* to do this to one another turned his stomach.

'They tore our power away and left us hollow and barren,' said Shai-Tan, as the lights blew out one by one. The chamber plunged into a shimmering twilight of warped psi-energy and crackling electricity.

To witness such a violation drained Magnus. It sapped his very soul.

'They took something beautiful and killed it...' he choked.

'They *thought* they killed it,' said Shai-Tan, 'but we endured. Tied to this place, but formless and adrift until finally we awoke. Once our tormentors finally understood what was happening, they fled their ship and warded it sealed, but they were too late. Their minds were already remade in our image. They became our heralds of the End Times. The seed-bearers of this world's doom.'

'The first Sons of Shai-Tan...' said Magnus.

The thing with Atharva's face nodded and easily lifted Magnus to slam him down on the surgical gurney. Unbreakable psychic force held him immobile as long-dormant mechanisms throbbed with returning power. Metal spun and twisted as the golden helm of the cranial restraint rotated around from beneath the gurney.

Shai-Tan leaned over Magnus as the machinery enfolded the primarch's head.

Spinning needles glittered. Electrodes sparked to life.

'You too will bear dreams of darkness beyond Morningstar,' said Shai-Tan. 'You shall be the brightest Son of Shai-Tan.'

TEN

MASSACRE • ROADS DIVERGE • AT WHAT COST?

Another four ships lifted off in quick succession, and Vashti let out a shuddering breath. Her heart rate hadn't dropped below a hundred in the last hour, and only the constant flow of stimms was keeping her going.

She gave herself a second to watch the departing contrails pushing up through the striated clouds overhead before turning her attention back to the hastily wired data-slates before her.

'The next wave is coming in too fast,' said Tessza Rom, her voice grating and mechanical.

'I see them,' she said, switching vox-channels. 'Flight Wave Six-Three Lambda, approaching on transit corridor Alpha-Niner, slow your approach. Cross demarcation line Olympia in five, four, three...'

She breathed a sigh of relief as she watched the tracks of the departing vessels and incoming craft diverge, no longer in danger of colliding.

'How many away in the last wave?' asked Vashti.

'Manifests record fifteen thousand en route to the fleet pickets.'

Vashti tapped the icons for the arriving craft and their hold volumes, working out how many people could be crammed inside.

'Not enough,' she said. 'It's never enough.'

She called the image of the tens of thousands pressed hard against the walls and gates of the fortress onto her tertiary slates. Her heart sank anew at the knowledge that most of these people would be left behind.

The approaching ships made a wide circuit of the fortress to bleed off the speed of their rapid descent. Vashti was put in mind of carrion feeders circling a corpse and preparing to pick clean its bones.

She shook off the disturbing image and her brow furrowed in puzzlement as she saw the newly arrived craft still hadn't begun their final approach.

'Tessza?' she said. 'What's going on? Why aren't those ships on their descent?'

'Checking now,' said Tessza. 'Flight Wave Six-Three Lambda, expedite your descent immediately. Our departure schedules allow for no delays. I repeat, commence your descent immediately.'

Vashti called up the passenger manifests. Thousands of names scrolled past, and she wondered how each name had been chosen. Who made the decision on who would live and who would die? Most likely it had been Perturabo, and in that moment Vashti hated him like she had hated no other living being. To stand over a world not his own and decide the fate of its people was the act of a tyrant.

An alert flashed onto her screen, and she swiped it to her primary panel. Trajectories flashed before her, downward spiralling patterns now reversing and heading back into orbit.

'What the...' she murmured, assuming it had to be an error.

She looked over at Tessza, seeing the magos twitching in her tank, the pink, gel-like amniotic fluid flecked with bubbles by her friend's consternation.

'Tessza?' she said. 'Why are those ships leaving?'

'They have been commanded to depart Calaena's airspace.'

'What?' said Vashti, checking her terminals for any sign of a command issued in error. 'Commanded by whom?'

'The command bears the seal of the Imperial governor,' said Tessza. 'It directs all ship captains to return to their carrier vessels and furthermore orders an immediate cessation of evacuation operations.'

'Is he insane?' demanded Vashti. 'We have days yet to evacuate the surface. We can save tens of thousands of Morningstar's people.'

A hard knot of dread formed in Vashti's gut at the thought of no more vessels returning to the surface. Was this the moment she had dreaded, the moment that those in charge decided that no more could be done?

'No, that makes no sense,' she said. 'This has to be a mistake. It's got to be.'

'The order is unambiguous,' said Tessza.

'I don't care how clear it is,' snapped Vashti. 'Rescind it! Get those damn ships back!'

'I am attempting to, but the captains refuse to return.'

'Then use the e-mag tether!' shouted Vashti. 'Get them down on these landing platforms right bloody now! Do what you have to do, but get them down and loading.'

Tessza's body flinched in its liquid suspension, and streams of noospheric data rose like red smoke from her tank.

'I cannot. I am locked out,' said Tessza, the artificial cadence of her voice still managing to convey indignation. 'None of our core systems are accepting my access codes.'

'How is that even possible?' asked Vashti, clearing her slates and going deep into the structure of the jury-rigged operating system the Mechanicum had set up for her aviation traffic-control protocols. She hadn't had time to perform due diligence on the minutiae of the system architecture. That they worked was enough for her.

To facilitate the evacuation efforts, the primarch Perturabo had consented to her cogitators being integrated with the logic engines of the Sharei Maveth, which meant she had access to the superior operating systems of the Iron Warriors fortress.

But that in turn meant anyone who could gain access to *her* system could access the fortress command network.

Lines of disrupting code bearing the authority seal of Konrad Vargha were copying themselves to every aspect of the citadel's internal systems, shutting down its defensive protocols one by one.

A series of juddering vibrations travelled up through the floor of the command centre, and Vashti turned to the slates displaying the exterior of the fortress. Her heart sank as she saw a number of enormous detonations rising skywards amongst the packed refugees. Panic spread through the thousands pressed up against the fortress wall as yet more explosions blasted deep craters in the ground.

'No, no, no, no!' she said, as the intricately layered and overlapping minefields began reactivating in deadly sequence. Dozens of explosions ripped through the tightly packed refugees, and Vashti bunched her fists as billowing clouds of smoke and debris obscured the full horror of the massacre. Shock waves travelled the full height of the wall and she wept to witness such an appalling death toll.

She would never know if what happened next was part of some monstrous plan or whether someone inside the Sharei Maveth acted with compassion for the victims beyond the wall.

The colossal gate of the fortress was rising.

And thousands of people poured inside.

Ahriman mag-locked his bolter to his thigh and moved to the eighth Enumeration. He wove a circle of perception in his hands and let his breath come in short, sharp hikes. He tapped into his Corvidae powers, enhancing the precognitive abilities of his brothers.

They fought in mandala formation, back to back and bolstering one another's abilities. A shield wall of psychic force deflected, absorbed and repelled the powers of their taken brothers and their nightmarish master.

Ahriman couldn't see Magnus, but he could feel his anguish.

Across the circle, Phosis T'kar was on his knees, grappling with M'eltan, one of the Athanaean Fellowship. M'eltan's body was aflame from head to toe. Smoke boiled from molten eye-lenses and from ruptured seams. Claws of fire were gouging through Phosis T'kar's armour as if it were soft butter.

Three other of Ahriman's brothers were dead, boiled alive inside their battleplate by Pavoni arts. Two more had been transformed into hideous, fused-black statues as chain lightning seared them to the deck. A kine-deflected mass-reactive bolt slammed Ahriman's pauldron, and fragments of its detonation tore at the surface of his helm. His vision fractured as an eye-lens cracked.

They fought in the eye of a hurricane formed of fire and lightning, held at bay by Raptora kine barriers. Flames ignited spilled chemicals and curdled the air with smoke. Blue-white arcs of electricity leapt and spat between the metal girders overhead.

Hollow laughter echoed from weeping shadows.

Thus far they had not employed any killing raptures, but their opponents were showing no such restraint. The six taken brothers of the Thousand Sons were blazing plumes of aetheric light, their power horrifically magnified by the disembodied souls sealed beneath Morningstar.

They were powerful, yes, but that power was a blunt instrument compared to the scalpel by which an adept of Prospero ought to wield such energy.

Ahriman ducked as a future echo pulsed in his mind.

A heavy metal gurney and its industrial-scale machinery slammed down where he had been standing, its mass driven by a hammerblow of kine force. It smashed three of his brothers from their feet. Two quickly got back in the fight; the third stayed down. Ahriman unleashed his own power in return and another of Shai-Tan's snared warriors flew back, slammed into a wall by the return strike.

He felt Phosis T'kar's pain and spun on his heel, thrusting his locked palms forwards. M'eltan staggered, but did not fall. The warrior turned and his gaze locked Ahriman in place. Ahriman stared into burning eyes like gateways to the abyss.

He was powerless against the depths of pain and suffering he saw there. M'eltan took a step towards him, lifting hands that burned with the atomic fire of newborn stars.

'Why do you fight us?' said M'eltan in a voice not his own.

Ahriman had no answer. Telepathic raptures gouged his mind, and their raw force was too great to resist. The sounds of battle receded and his urge to fight diminished as the fiery being walking towards him seemed less like a monster, more like an angel of blazing beauty.

His death would be wondrous.

A kine-wreathed fist exploded from M'eltan's chest as Phosis T'kar surged to his feet with a roar of anger. Augmented with power from the Great Ocean, the blow obliterated M'eltan's torso. Gobbets of brilliant fire exploded from the impact, and Phosis T'kar slumped against a bulkhead glittering with psychic hoarfrost.

'I could have taken him,' gasped Phosis T'kar, 'but thank you for the distraction.'

Ahriman let out a heaving breath as the attack on his mind ceased and his psychic defences threw off M'eltan's raptures. The sounds of battle surged within his skull – the roar of flames, the crackle of lightning, the hard bangs of mass-reactive rounds.

The pain of the dying.

The fury of the dead.

'You killed him...' he said at last, kneeling by the smouldering ruin of M'eltan's remains.

'Of course I did,' said Phosis T'kar, drawing fresh power into his body. 'And you're a fool if you think we're going to get out of here without killing.'

'He was our brother,' said Ahriman, as the full horror of what Phosis T'kar had done sank in. 'You killed a fellow legionary of the Fifteenth...'

Ahriman tried to look away from the broken remains of his brother, but the terrible significance of what Phosis T'kar had done was too great. He reached down and placed both palms in M'eltan's steaming blood.

'When we kill one another it is the beginning of the end,' said Ahriman, as a host of jagged images ripped through his mind.

Broken ceramite, ten thousand bolters firing in unison on a world of black sand, a howling wolf beneath a four-faced moon, blood enough to drown the galaxy...

He stared at the rich redness coating his palms. The blood on his hands dripped from his fingertips, and he knew with terrible certainty that this would not be the last of his brothers that he saw murdered by one of their own.

'This is where our road diverges,' said Ahriman.

'Damn Corvidae,' said Phosis T'kar, reloading his bolter with fresh shells. 'So worried about the future, you forget to live in the now. Come on, fight! There're enemies all around! Look!'

Ahriman shook off the grotesque images of slaughter as another vision filled his skull. He saw Magnus held down on a metal gurney, convulsing as a helm of gold isolated him from the heart of his power.

A sudden stillness and a moment of silence isolated Ahriman.

He heard a voice whisper into his mind.

+My favoured son...+

'I hear you,' said Ahriman, turning and feeling a heart filled with regret and guilt coming from deeper into the chamber. The urge to break the mandala was overpowering, though it fought against every aspect of his training that told him to maintain it.

'What did you say?' said Phosis T'kar.

'I have to go to him,' said Ahriman.

'Who?'

'Our father. He spoke to me.'

Phosis T'kar heard Ahriman's certainty and nodded.

'Spearhead!' he yelled, and the Thousand Sons transitioned swiftly into their assault formation: a fighting wedge of ceramite and steel, a thrust of psychic might and genhanced strength.

Ahriman took position at the tip of the spear as Hathor Maat – or, rather, the thing that wore his flesh – stepped from a corona of psychic fire. Power haloed his brother, crude in comparison to what the true Hathor Maat could wield, but potent nonetheless.

'Pavoni power in the wind,' yelled Phosis T'kar.

Ahriman felt a sickening ache in his marrow, a restless ambition within his flesh. A fist of nausea clenched his gut as his cells responded to the mutant urge encoded in the earliest stages of their being.

He willed his flesh to stillness, but the corpses hanging from the shattered cryo-tubes had no such imperative to resist. Rotten, centuries-dead meat jerked to spasmodic life as aether energy suffused glossy, jellied limbs.

One by one, the sodden corpses pulled free from their shattered glass tubes, held aloft by the psychic strings of a mad puppeteer. The light of the Great Ocean burned in gaping eye sockets, and dead fluids drooled from slack jaws.

Hundreds of the resurrected surrounded them, and more were lurching from their cryo-tubes with every passing moment.

'Bloody Pavoni,' sighed Phosis T'kar.

Neon-bright pillars of radiance pierced the sky and etched themselves against the darkness. The clouds burned to vapour as collimated beams of orbital weaponry banished night and illuminated Morningstar for a thousand kilometres in all directions.

The orbital barrage fell in a cascade of macro-lasers and atomic fire. As with everything the Iron Warriors did, it was relentless, thorough and merciless.

Perturabo felt the shock waves from the destruction of the world-killing machinery a second after the flash dimmed the glass of the Stormbird's canopy. The gunship shuddered as the toroidal pressure wave sought to tear it from the sky.

He gripped the control column and kept them pointed back towards Calaena as a continental-scale firestorm ignited over what remained of the planet's oceans.

'To unleash such devastation usually brings me a sense of vindication,' said Perturabo, 'a sense that some great evil had been defeated.'

'You don't feel that?' asked Barban Falk.

'No, I feel nothing. This has achieved nothing.'

'We knew that going in,' pointed out Falk.

'I knew this vengeance would be symbolic, but I still assumed I would feel a measure of satisfaction at striking back.'

'And you don't?'

'No, because we have already lost this fight. It was lost before we even made planetfall. Our enemies on Morningstar are beyond my ability to punish. To kill them would only fulfil their desire to die.'

'Then what are we to do?'

'We save as many innocents as we can, then leave this world and never look back.'

Falk nodded and turned back to the console as urgent comm-chatter sparked over the vox. The storms and electromagnetic fallout from the orbital barrage made sifting the signal from the interference next to impossible, but Barban Falk was a master at extracting meaning from chaos.

His fingers danced over the controls, and howling interference filled the cockpit until the voice of Harkor was rendered in scratching, wavering static.

'... *under attack... breached the gates. The bastards are inside the Sharei Maveth! Systems failing throughout... no... thousands of them. Don't... preparing to fight–'*

The transmission was abruptly cut off and Perturabo and Falk shared a look of disbelief that an Iron Warriors fortress could have been breached by mortals.

'Remember everything I just said about our enemies being beyond our ability to punish?'

'Yes?' said Falk.

'I was wrong,' said Perturabo. 'These bastards will pay in blood for this, and I am going to enjoy every second of it.'

The golden helm enclosed Magnus' head and he felt the touch of electrodes at his temples. They buzzed with current. His mouth filled with moisture. He tasted metal.

'You don't need to do this,' he said, as a host of needles pressed through his hair to prick his scalp.

'Everyone who lies on these slabs says that,' said Shai-Tan.

'You don't – I can help you.'

'How is it you think you can help us?' said Shai-Tan, the light of its rage burning in Atharva's eyes. 'Can you imagine the obscenity of what was done here? Thousands of innocents, whose only crime was to be born capable of miracles, were stripped of their uniqueness. Many did not survive the process, but those that did soon wished they had died. Imagine a painter losing his eyes overnight, a virtuoso musician shattering the bones in her hands or a singer with the most sublime voice struck dumb. That is what they did to us, and you think you can *help?*'

Magnus let Shai-Tan's words wash through him, their remembered pain breaking his heart. He sifted the myriad splintered moments for a singular truth, searching for a way to free Atharva and the others, a way to undo what had been done here.

He closed his eye, letting his mind absorb Shai-Tan's pain, reliving it over and over through the memories of all those who had suffered here. When he opened it again, it was to see an echo of the past...

The medicae chamber was as it had once been, pristine white and sterile, a place of terrible psychic surgery.

Magnus looked up through the memory of the woman who had lain on this gurney before him. He wept as he experienced her terror and incomprehension at what was being done. Anonymous men in protective suits of vulcanised rubber, wearing rebreather masks and obscuring visors, loomed over her. They bore needles and psychically caustic drugs.

He gagged on the plastek mouth guard intended to keep her from biting her tongue. He thrashed as they fitted burning needles and clamps to her head. He clawed at their faces and managed to pull clear the mask of her nearest tormentor. Magnus looked into his unremarkable features, seeing not the face of a monster, but a frightened, guilty man.

Magnus plunged deep into this man's mind, learning everything about him in the space of a breath – his hopes and his dreams, and everything that made him human. But the truth of mortal minds lay not in their dreams, but coiled in their fears.

What terrors had consumed the settlers of this world...?

And the answer to the question he had posed to Perturabo when they began their mission to Morningstar was starkly clear.

Magnus released his hold on the woman's memories of past horror and flew back to the present, drawing a great draught of chemical-rich air into his lungs. Pain throbbed at his temples and glacial cold filled his immobile limbs.

The electrodes within the golden helm pulsed with burning current, blackening the skin beneath. Wetness coated his scalp as the rotating needles eased inwards, millimetre by millimetre. His thoughts were sluggish. The low-level buzz of insects filled his skull.

Magnus bit back the pain. 'I know why they did this to you.'

'Because they feared us,' snapped Shai-Tan. 'And because fear leads to hate, they stripped us of our abilities.'

'No,' said Magnus. 'That wasn't it. That wasn't it at all.'

'Then why?' demanded Shai-Tan. 'Tell me why they did this to us, why they let so many of us die, screaming in terror, or left broken and mad? Tell me what *reason* could possibly have justified all this?'

'*Old Night...*' gasped Magnus as the needles met the resistance of bone.

'Old Night?' said Shai-Tan.

'An age of strife and bloodshed like nothing seen before,' said Magnus. 'A wave of mass insanity that swept through human space, consuming entire worlds in a galactic extinction event.'

The electrodes were burning Magnus' skin, the needles boring into his skull. He felt the sting of the psychoactive chemicals at their tips begin to spread into his bloodstream.

How much longer did he have before his thought processes became too disconnected to reach Shai-Tan?

'Humanity was evolving too quickly,' he said. 'The emergence of so many with the psyker gene was too sudden, too drastic. It could only end in disaster. The mass insanity... It manifested through the psykers, infecting whole worlds and plunging them into an abyss of ruin and death.'

'No...' said Shai-Tan.

'What they did here? It was terrible and monstrous and beyond all reach of morality, yes, but it made Morningstar a world without psykers. The killing madness never took hold in this place. It had no way in, no victims to infect. The planet's populace were *immune*. Old Night never fell.'

'You lie,' said Shai-Tan.

'Look inside my mind. See for yourself.'

Shai-Tan stepped back, its stolen features twisted in dawning comprehension. Magnus felt its fury ebb, before it surged back, more ferocious than ever.

'They saved the world,' said Magnus.

'At the cost of our lives!' shouted Shai-Tan.

'When you love something with every fragment of your soul, you will sacrifice *anything* to save it.'

'Anything?' said Shai-Tan.

'Anything. Trust me on this,' said Magnus, before roaring in pain as the full power of the ancient machinery shrieked within the vault of his skull.

It was unlike anything he had experienced or could have imagined. It burned the meat of his mind, cauterising delicate psychic nodes and disrupting synaptic networks of arcane configurations.

Magnus spasmed as the very essence of what made him unique amongst his brothers was drawn out of his mind like blood from a vein. The edges of the world grew dimmer, less vivid and defined. To see the world as those without seersight saw it filled Magnus with gut-wrenching horror.

Shai-Tan gripped his throat, as if seeking to choke the life from him as well as sever him from his power, a maddened god exacting pain for pain, as if the scales could ever be balanced.

Magnus fought against the force holding him down, his agony and the terror of being without his power lending strength to his limbs. His hand clamped around Atharva's gorget and he squeezed. The metal and ceramite cracked, but Shai-Tan only increased the pressure on his neck.

Locked together in a lethal embrace, they were beings with the power of gods fighting a battle to the death: neither willing to surrender, both willing to meet their end.

Movement caught Magnus' eye, blurred and hazed by pain and the ruptured capillaries misting his vision with blood. He saw kine blades rising and falling, whipping arcs of psionic light, warriors in crimson plate awash with smoke and blazing auras. A host of dead, pallid-skinned golems surrounded them.

Leading them was a warrior wreathed in amber fire, his radiance like that of the pious saints depicted on the ceilings of ancient temples.

'Ahzek...' gasped Magnus. 'My favoured son...'

Ahriman charged Shai-Tan, firing his bolter from the hip before reaching for his combat blade when the slide racked back on an empty breech.

Shai-Tan looked up and lifted one of his hands from Magnus' neck. A pale nimbus of light, like the glow of the dawn's first star, built around his fingers and exploded outwards in a series of spiralling comets.

The explosive psychic impact filled the chamber with blinding light. Magnus cried out as Ahriman was tossed through the air to land limply across one of the slabs. He looked up into Atharva's face, seeing ethereal masks of spite-filled souls revelling in the pain they had caused.

Ahriman's assault had achieved only a momentary distraction, but it was all the opening that Magnus needed.

Resolve settled in his bones, resolve he had known he lacked until now.

'I will save you,' he said, wrenching his other hand free to tear loose Shai-Tan's grip on his neck. 'If you let me.'

A kine pulse of thought pushed the needles from his skull and Magnus sat bolt upright as Shai-Tan recoiled.

'Your power is great, but it is undisciplined,' he said, twisting Atharva's wrist and snapping it with a sickening crack of bone. The souls within Atharva screamed at this reversal. Magnus rolled and shrugged Atharva from him like a brawler pinning his opponent to the floor.

He held Atharva to the slab, one hand around his neck, the other poised in a fist above him.

'I am Magnus, Master of Prospero, and I was taught by the Emperor of Man, the greatest psyker in the galaxy,' he said, looking deep within Shai-Tan. 'Against that, you have *nothing!*'

Atharva's body convulsed beneath him, wild psychic energy contorting his limbs in unnatural ways as Shai-Tan fought Magnus' iron discipline. He felt fury snapping at him, an eternal anger that knew no forgiveness. Magnus nodded, as if coming to a solemn decision within himself.

'I am sorry, my son,' he said. 'There is no other way.'

The golden helm snapped down over Atharva's head and shimmered with power as the needles punched deep into his skull.

'Hold to your silver cord!' cried Magnus as a looming vision of a dreadful, faceless angel burned itself on his mind. 'Hold fast to it and never let go, or it will be your end.'

Magnus closed his eye, but could not cut himself off from the awful sound of his son's pain and fear. He heard the drilling needles pierce bone and felt the burning horror of the chemicals, neuro-scramblers and gemynd-shears doing their grisly work within Atharva's skull.

Shai-Tan screamed as it once again endured the agonies that had birthed it, the horror of being torn from a body of flesh and blood. It fled Atharva and surged into the aether as a billowing storm of hate and fury. Magnus saw it as a swirling red maelstrom, a daemon of nightmare taking shape in a psychic storm that burned the air with its fury.

He had been waiting for Shai-Tan to abandon its host and stood before its swelling storm fury with one arm thrust forwards, the other flat upon the great grimoire chained to his waist.

Shai-Tan howled and the deck plates buckled with its violence. Magnus remained upright as hurricane winds of psychic force sought to dash him against the walls. He rooted himself to the spot, an immoveable object in the face of irresistible force.

'What happened here was unforgivable,' said Magnus. 'I promise it will be remembered. You will *all* be remembered.'

He thrust his grimoire towards Shai-Tan's essence and its cover of red leather flew open like a portal to other worlds. Shai-Tan shrieked and fought against the pull of the Book of Magnus, but the grimoire's depthless thirst for learning was like an irresistible ocean vortex.

'All who died in these halls will live again,' promised Magnus. 'Let go of the hate and you will be born anew in a realm of limitless imagination.'

The strongest souls within Shai-Tan's essence resisted, unwilling to let go of their hatred, but more and more were accepting Magnus' offer with every passing second.

Magnus drew them all into the book – a litany of names and lives, a record of the dead and the forgotten. He was their conduit, and he experienced their lives in the space of a heartbeat as he offered them a future.

And pages replete with ancient tales of magic and legends were enriched with a new cast of characters, fresh players to strut upon the stages of strange and mythical lands. Within the pages of Magnus' book, the stolen souls of Morningstar would live incredible lives and experience untold adventure.

The cover of the book slammed shut and the hurricane winds vanished in an instant. Magnus let out a shuddering breath and sank to his knees as sudden stillness fell across the chamber.

The bodies of the dead and his enslaved sons fell to the deck, now freed from Shai-Tan's controlling force.

'My lord?' said a voice, and Magnus looked up to see Ahzek Ahriman staring at him. 'Is it over?'

Magnus placed a hand upon his grimoire and thought of what he had learned in his connection to Shai-Tan. His shoulders slumped, as if the greatest burden imaginable had just been placed upon him.

'No,' he said. 'There is one last dark deed before us.'

'What dark deed?' asked Ahriman.

'To finish what was begun,' said Magnus.

EPILOGUE

Refugee vessels glittered in the light of the doomed world, an ad-hoc fleet of well over a thousand ships of all sizes and displacement. It was a fleet of desperation, every vessel packed with the indigenous survivors of Morningstar. Shuttles still ferried people back and forth, segregating natives from non-natives.

Magnus and Perturabo watched from the command deck of the *Iron Blood* as Legion vessels manoeuvred around the fleet like shepherds guarding a flock from predators.

Perturabo's flagship was a place of functionality, yet its arches were gracefully formed over latticed ironwork. Magnus recognised many of the decorative flourishes from the plans he had seen etched on wax paper in his brother's workshop.

Warriors in burnished plate stood at their command stations like iron sculptures, ready to enact their primarch's orders the instant they were given. No one spoke. The only sound was the buzz of cogitators and the constant thrum of the engines through the deck plates.

Perturabo's armour was still bloody from the fighting in the Sharei Maveth and still radiated heat from action. It had taken all Magnus' considerable powers of persuasion to convince

Perturabo to abandon his fortress. It railed against every fibre of his brother's soul to leave a fight unfinished, and the look in his eyes when they met atop the landing platforms of the embattled fortress told Magnus the matter lay between them like an impassable gulf.

Forrix and Harkor's squads had held the gates to the upper levels while the Iron Warriors and Thousand Sons evacuated the Sharei Maveth. And with every gunship that blasted into orbit, Magnus felt a little of his brother's love for him diminish.

Barban Falk had emerged from the fighting, dragging the bloodied, struggling form of Konrad Vargha behind him. At first Magnus thought the warrior was rescuing him, but then he read the truth of the situation in the man's aura.

'He wants to die,' Falk said, tossing the weeping, soiled governor onto the bloodied floor of a gunship. 'But he's going to live, alone and in chains in an iron cell for the rest of his life.'

Vashti Eshkol and Tessza Rom had escaped on a battered Mechanicum tender, angry and bewildered at being forced to leave Morningstar while there were yet people to save. Niko Ashkali was secured aboard a XV Legion gunship, still recovering from her ordeal of being stranded at Zharrukin.

Magnus' last sight of Morningstar's surface had been of a world tearing itself apart, of a city engulfed in madness and of jeering traitors standing atop the flaming bastions of his brother's fortress.

This was not how I saw this ending.

He took a breath, realising that Perturabo had spoken to him.

'What?' he said, looking into the cold, flinty eyes of his brother.

'I asked if you're absolutely sure about this?'

'I am sure,' said Magnus. 'Throne, I wish I was not.'

Perturabo sighed. 'And you said *I* had a cruel streak.'

'This is not cruelty.'

'Only if you're right.'

'I am.'

Perturabo sneered. 'Always so certain.'

'It has to be this way,' replied Magnus, placing a protective hand over the book chained at his waist. 'It is the only way to be sure no seeds of Shai-Tan's apocalyptic vision are allowed to flower elsewhere. Remember, I saw inside it. I saw how deep its hate runs.'

Perturabo folded his arms. 'Bitter experience has taught my Legion to bear moments like this. Can you say the same of yours?'

'You have no idea what my Legion can bear,' said Magnus.

'Perhaps not, but this will scar them forever.'

'Scars heal,' said Magnus.

'But they leave a mark. Your sons will remember this.'

'They have endured worse,' said Magnus, lost in black memory of screams and warriors begging to die. 'They will forget this as they forgot that.'

He sensed Perturabo's puzzlement, but did not elaborate. Now was not the time for reminiscing over past sins.

'Do it,' he said.

Perturabo nodded to his Iron Warriors. 'Open fire.'

The *Iron Blood* shuddered as every one of its weapon batteries unleashed hell. The vessels of both Legions followed suit, illuminating the void with murderous ordnance and killing fire from a thousand guns.

Magnus forced himself to watch as the refugee fleet burned, every last ship gutted by endless broadsides of macro-cannons, lances and wave after wave of atomic torpedoes. The barrage continued for two hours until nothing remained.

The wreckage tumbled back to Morningstar's surface as world-ending weapons of Exterminatus fell from orbit.

'All is dust,' said Magnus.

The Planet of the Sorcerers
Time unknown

'I still hear the dead of Morningstar screaming,' said Magnus, clawing a handful of ash from the crater within the Pyramid of Photep. Cold winds blew around him, spiteful zephyrs blowing in between the vast and twisted spars of the buckled structure.

'*We* are the dead of Morningstar.'

Magnus let the ash fall from his fingers and looked up.

The power that once wore the face of Atharva beneath Morningstar was transformed. Its face changed with each blink, every breath. It was a man, a woman, old and young, every race and colour.

'You look different,' he said.

'This is a world where the only constant is inconstancy.'

'I ought to have left you on Morningstar,' said Magnus, brushing the dust and glass around him.

'Perhaps,' said Shai-Tan, looking out over the fallen beauty and shattered ruins of Tizca. 'But Magnus the Red can never resist the call of knowledge, even when he knows it should be left alone.'

'Your pain was so deep,' said Magnus, making fists in the dust, his knuckles grating on metal. 'I felt what they did to you and

I was moved to pity. I was a weak, naive fool. You damned a world as vengeance for your pain. Of all the souls to escape Morningstar's destruction, why was it yours?'

'Because you look to save what cannot be saved, to undo what cannot be undone,' said Shai-Tan, kneeling before him. 'That is your weakness. What was it you said? "When you love something with every fragment of your soul..."'

'You will sacrifice anything to save it,' finished Magnus.

'Tell me, what would you sacrifice to cheat fate and save your sons?'

'My life,' said Magnus without hesitation.

'You gave that on Prospero,' said Shai-Tan. 'What else?'

'I have nothing else to offer.'

Shai-Tan joined him in sweeping dust and glass from the crater. 'There is a way to take yourself from the board, to remove your sons from the sight of hungry gods.'

Magnus nodded slowly and cast his mind back to the aftermath of his abandonment of Morningstar.

'I remember transferring from the *Iron Blood* to the *Photep* and watching the life-eater virus spread over the planet's surface. I watched toxins turn what was once a verdant world of blue and gold and green to a necrotic mass of brown and mottled purple. But even that vanished when the *Photep* fired a lance strike to ignite the atmosphere and begin the global firestorm.'

'Such apocalyptic endings have become more common of late,' said Shai-Tan. 'If you hope I will mourn Morningstar's doom, you will be disappointed.'

'I do not hope for that,' said Magnus.

'Then do you tell of it because that was not your last sight of Morningstar?' said Shai-Tan. 'I felt your return, many years after the life-eater was dead. How could I not? You descended to the surface and excavated Zharrukin's ruins.'

'Yes.'

'To find the arcane machinery aboard the *Shai-Tan*?'

Magnus nodded. 'Yes.'

'So the tale is not complete?'

'No tale is ever complete,' said Magnus. 'The time you spent in my grimoire should have taught you that. As one story ends, another unfolds.'

'And as death follows life, so rebirth follows death,' said Shai-Tan, kneeling beside Magnus to sweep the last of the debris from the base of the crater.

Though Magnus had known what he would see, the sight of the rusted hatch and its armourglass portal still took his breath away. Emblazoned at the centre of the hatch was a vectored arrow, encircled by a stylised circle and wreath.

The sigil of Morningstar.

'No,' he said, pushing himself to his feet. 'I was wrong – there is no rebirth to be had below in that place of horror.'

'There will be,' said Shai-Tan. 'One day.'

'I will never open that damned ship,' said Magnus.

'No, your favoured son will open it when you cast him aside, and he has nowhere left to turn,' said Shai-Tan. 'When he will show you how wrong you have been all this time.'

The echo of the Emperor's words sent a shiver of dark prescience through Magnus.

He glimpsed a lightning-wreathed tower, a cabal of sorcerers…
Betrayal and death in equal measure.

Magnus turned and walked away as Shai-Tan called after him.

'All will be dust, Magnus. All will be dust.'

He did not turn back.

ABOUT THE AUTHOR

Graham McNeill has written many Horus Heresy novels, including *Vengeful Spirit* and his *New York Times* bestsellers *A Thousand Sons* and the novella *The Reflection Crack'd*, which featured in *The Primarchs* anthology. Graham's Ultramarines series, featuring Captain Uriel Ventris, is now six novels long, and has close links to his Iron Warriors stories, the novel *Storm of Iron* being a perennial favourite with Black Library fans. He has also written a Mars trilogy, featuring the Adeptus Mechanicus. For Warhammer, he has written the Time of Legends trilogy *The Legend of Sigmar*, the second volume of which won the 2010 David Gemmell Legend Award.

THE HORUS HERESY®
PRIMARCHS

CHRIS WRAIGHT

LEMAN RUSS

THE GREAT WOLF

An extract from
LEMAN RUSS:
THE GREAT WOLF
by Chris Wraight

Haldor pressed himself against frigid stone, rough-cut and slick with ice. He took in a deep breath, enjoying the searing cold in his lungs. The dark pressed around him, just as it had in the forests of Asaheim, blue-black, vengeful.

Then he was moving again, loping like he had done before, deeper down. He did not know all the ways of the Mountain yet. Perhaps no Sky Warrior did, for the fortress was never more than a fraction full. The great bulk of the Chapter was forever at war, coming back to the home world only for feasts or councils, and in any case the place had been intended for a Legion.

He went on, further away, deeper down. The echoes of mortal voices died away entirely, replaced by the almost imperceptible rhythm of the deep earth. Ice cracked endlessly, ticking like a chrono in the dark. Meltwater, formed over buried power lines, trickled across broken stone before freezing again in swirling patterns below. From the great shafts came the half-audible growls of the massive reactors tended by the Iron Priests, and the eternal forges that created the Chapter's weapons of war, and, so he had heard tell, the forgotten halls where the eldest of all dwelt, their hearts locked in ice and their minds kept in a stasis of dreams.

By then he had no idea where he was going, nor why, only that the shadows were welcome, and for the moment he had no need of fire to warm his hearts nor more flesh to fill his innards. He had been changed, and his body embraced the crippling cold where once it would have killed him, and he welcomed it.

Then he froze, and the hairs on the back of his arms lifted. Soundlessly, swift as a thought, he reached for the haft of the axe bound at his belt.

The corridor ahead was as dark and empty as all the others, rising slightly and curving to the left. Haldor narrowed his gaze, but the shadow lay heavy, and nothing broke the gloom.

Something was there, up ahead, out of visual range but detectable all the same. A pheromone, perhaps, or the ghost of a scent. Haldor dropped low and crept forwards, keeping the haft gripped loose. The tunnels of the Fang were full of dangers, all knew that. He became painfully aware of how noisy his armour was, and how much stealthier he could be without it.

He reached the curve ahead and passed around it. The change in the air told him the corridor had opened out, but the dark was now unbroken. He could hear something out there – breathing, like an animal's, soft and low – but could not pin it down. He crouched, shifting the weight of the axe, readying to move.

Before he could do anything more, a voice came out of the darkness, deeper than any animal's, rimed with age.

'Put the axe down, lad.'

Haldor had obeyed before he even knew it, bound by a gene-heritage that was older than he was. Suddenly, the pall seemed to shift, and a figure loomed up through the Fang's under-murk. For a moment, all Haldor saw was a figment of old race-nightmares – a daemon of the darkling woods, crowned with branches, eyes as blue as sea-ice and hands like the gnarled roots of trees.

But then he was looking into features he knew as well as his own, despite never having seen them in flesh and blood. The face was smeared with ashes, a daub-pattern of black on pale skin. A heavy mantle of furs hung over hunched shoulders, and a gunmetal-grey gauntlet clutched at the hilt of a heavy, rune-encrusted longsword.

Instantly, without being bidden, Haldor dropped to one knee.

'Enough of that,' said his primarch, testily. 'Why are you here?'

Haldor didn't know. Aeska's words had driven him out, and the cold had sucked him in, but that was all he understood. Perhaps it had been the drink, or perhaps the last chance to walk the silent depths before war called, or maybe the tug of fate.

Now he stood, alone, in the presence of the Lord of Winter and War.

'One of Aeska's whelps,' said Leman Russ, drawing closer, his strange eyes shining in the dark. 'No wonder you left the hall. Bloody sagas. I've heard them all.'

Haldor couldn't tell if he was jesting. 'They told of the Allfather,' he said, hesitantly, wary of the danger in the primarch's every move. Russ was like a blackmane: huge, unpredictable, bleeding with danger. 'They said you fought Him. The only time you lost.'

Russ barked out a laugh, and the fur mantle shook. 'Not the only time.' He shrank back into the shadows then, seeming to diminish a fraction, but the danger remained.

Haldor caught snatched glimpses of his master's garb. Not the heavy armour plate of the warrior-king, but layers of hard-spun wool, streaked with the charcoal of spent embers. They were the clothes of death rites, of mourning. Some warrior of the Aett, perhaps even the *Einherjar,* must have been slain, though it was unusual for the Wolf Priests not to have called out the names of the dead through the Chapter.

Russ noticed the weapon Haldor had placed back at his belt,

and looked at it strangely. 'You know what blade that is?' he asked.

Haldor shook his head, and Russ snorted in disgust.

'The gaps grow, holes in the ice, greater with every summer-melt,' the primarch said. 'You know nothing. They remember nothing.'

Russ trailed off, half turning back towards the dark. Haldor said nothing. His hearts were both beating, a low thud, an instinctive threat-response even when no blades were raised.

'I know not whether you were sent to mock me or bring me comfort,' Russ said at last, 'but sent you were. So listen. Listen and remember.'

Haldor stayed where he was, not daring to move, watching the huge, fur-clad outline under the Mountain's heart. Russ was speaking like a skjald.

'I fought the Allfather, that is true, and He bested me, for the gods themselves fear Him, mightiest of men. But that was not the only time.'

The eyes shone, points of sapphire, lost in the grip of ice-shadow.

'There was another.'

Order the novel or download the eBook
from *blacklibrary.com*
Also available from